BETTER OFF BREAD

COMPASS COVE COZY MYSTERY BOOK 3

MARA WEBB

CHAPTER 1

"Look I'm telling you; I am *not* crazy! She was there, in the mirror! I saw her! It was mom. Our mom!"

Zelda looked at me as if I *was* crazy. "Look Zora, I believe you, but—"

"But there's no three ways about it," my familiar Hermes pitched in as he unexpectedly crawled out of my handbag. "You sound crazier than a coconut right about now." Both Zelda and I stared at Hermes for a second as he hopped onto one of the chairs in the waiting room.

"Great, now he's here too—for some reason," I flustered.

"Nice to see you too," Hermes said smarmily. "Also, it's not my fault you don't check your handbag before you go places."

"It's a *handbag,* I kind of figured I didn't have to check it for sleeping cats."

"First of all, it *is* a handbag. Who doesn't check their bag before they leave?"

"He's got a point," Zelda said.

I glared at her. "You can shove a sock in it!"

"Second of all," Hermes continued. "That handbag is silk-lined. It's one of my new favorite nap spots."

"That handbag was less than ten dollars, and I bought it from a supermarket, there's no way it's silk-lined." In fact, that wasn't even the whole truth. I'd found the handbag in a dumpster several years ago one night when I was walking back from work. I wasn't exactly a habitual dumpster diver, that had actually been my first time, but the bag was too pretty to pass up. Why would someone throw away a perfectly good handbag like that?

"Well maybe it's some sort of hybrid polyester blend, I don't know, I don't care, all I know is that is feels divine on my silky behind."

"Too much information," Zelda and I both said at the same time.

"Are we at Doctor Yamgov's?" Hermes said, widening his eyes and looking around the waiting room for the first time. "Ooh boy, she really does think you're crazy, Zora!"

I looked at Zelda in despair. "Wait a second, what exactly are we doing here? I thought you said this guy knew something about mom."

"He might! But I thought it wouldn't hurt to... get a checkup."

"What?!"

The situation was this: Both Zelda and I grew up separately without our mother. Mom disappeared shortly after I was born, and not long after that she had my younger sister Zelda with a different man. Not long after *that* mom disappeared completely, and she'd been missing ever since.

Three days ago I had seen my mother's reflection in my bathroom mirror, after spotting it the reflection immediately ran out of view. To a normal person this *would* absolutely be crazy, but I was a witch, so the realms of the unbelievable were a little more blurred for my kind.

After telling my sister and the rest of the witches in my family what I'd seen, they'd all received the information with awkwardly polite smiles, like they were entertaining the crazed ramblings of the local lunatic.

We were now sitting in a waiting room of a local magical doctor. Zelda told me this guy might possibly know more about our mother, as he was her doctor before she went missing—but now it seemed she had brought me here on false pretenses.

"You brought me here to get me checked up?!" I bellowed.

"Keep your voice down!" Zelda whispered frantically.

I looked around the empty waiting room in exasperation. "Or what? More flaking paint is going to peel off the walls? What is this place anyway?! It looks like it's been abandoned for the better part of sixty years!"

Doctor Yamgov's practice was, for lack of a better word, baffling. It literally looked like it had last been decorated in the 1950s, the walls were covered in this flaking sickly green paint, the lights overhead cast an unsettling yellow light over every surface, and the floors were covered in huge black and white square tiles that felt very clinical.

The building's interior was a liminal labyrinth, endless staircases and hallways that were very confusing to navigate. From the outside Doctor Yamgov's clinic, which was set amongst a row of brownstone townhouses, looked like a normal enough building. Things got confusing when you stepped inside though—and the longer I spent in this waiting room the less I wanted to be here.

"Look Yamgov is eccentric, but he's really one of the best doctors in Compass Cove. He knows every magical ailment like the back of his hand!" Zelda said.

"Be straight with me," I said. "You didn't bring me here because this guy knows about mom, you brought me here because you think I'm going crazy. All because I said I saw mom in the mirror! Aren't we witches? Last I checked seeing weird things in mirrors isn't that crazy!"

"It's uh... pretty crazy," Hermes piped up. I looked at him.

"What did you say?"

"Look I know you're still new to this whole witch business," he said, "but I can't sit here and let you embarrass yourself."

"What are you talking about?" I asked, suddenly feeling a little self-conscious.

"Look Zora, if you say you saw your mother in the mirror then I believe you, but—"

"But what?" I asked.

Hermes sighed. "I was Constance's familiar for a long time. I didn't know your mother—I didn't know Tabitha *that* well because she was a bit of a recluse, but I did know her. Just before Tabitha really went off the deep end she developed this fascination with mirrors, a fascination that quickly turned into an all-consuming phobia."

"...What?" I said. "Why has no one told me until now?" I looked at Zelda.

"Don't look at me, I know nothing about her!" she protested.

"I didn't mention it because it's inconsequential," Hermes said. "Your mother was a mad woman, Zora, I'm not going to go around talking about every little crazy thing I'd heard her say, because then *I'd* sound mad. Besides, I don't know why you're getting so aggressive with me, I'm on your side here, a mental health checkup is completely unnecessary."

"Thank you!" I said, jabbing my hand in Hermes direction. "Finally, a little support."

"I didn't finish," Hermes pipped. "It's not necessary because it's already obvious that you're a fruitcake. You and *her*." Hermes nodded at Zelda. "Mad as two boxes of frogs, both of you."

"Rich coming from the guy that sleeps in handbags," Zelda muttered.

"You know what, I don't need this disrespect!" Hermes shouted starkly. He was a great diva whenever he wanted to be. "I thought I'd tagalong for a little adventure, but no, I can tell when I'm not welcome!" Hermes hopped down from the chair and started walking away from us.

"And where are you going to go?" I asked. "I don't think I've seen you walk further than a room's length since I moved here."

"I have my tricks!" he shouted. With that a small smoking doorway no bigger than a cat flap opened on the wall ahead of him and Hermes walked through. As the tip of his tail vanished out of sight the door disappeared. I turned to look at Zelda and saw that her mouth was hanging open.

"Did you know he could do that?" I asked.

"No... no I did not."

Someone shouted from across the waiting room then, making us both jump. "Wick!?"

Looking over I saw a bony old man in a doctor's coat. His head was a mess of frizzy white hair, and upon his face a pair of goggles magnified his eyes to the size of teacups.

"...Yes?" I hazarded.

"Well come on then, I haven't got all day!" he snapped.

"Right, of course," I muttered uncertainly. I rose to my feet and looked at Zelda, who was still sitting. "Coming?"

"It's your appointment, not mine!"

"You too, Zelda!" Yamgov bellowed. "Mental illness runs in your family. Might as well get you checked up too!"

Zelda opened her mouth, her expression indicating that she thought this highly unfair. Yamgov turned on his heel and walked back through the door from which he'd come, clearly done waiting on us.

I grinned at Zelda and pulled her to her feet. "Look at that, we have a joint appointment! He's got a point Zel." I took my sister's arm and we marched forward to Doctor Yamgov's office. "If I'm crazy... you're probably crazy too!"

"Stupid family ties..." Zelda muttered to herself as we passed through the door.

* * *

"WELL THE GOOD news is that neither of you are crazy," Doctor Yamgov said after putting us through various magical tests, all of which were highly unusual. Despite looking like a mad scientist from an old monster movie Yamgov himself was relatively normal, if a little eccentric. He sat down in and old leather chair, steepled his hands together and stared at the two of us curiously, his thick white eyebrows poised at different levels on his wrinkled forehead. "Tell me then, why do you think you're crazy?"

"I *don't* think I'm crazy." I shot a glance at Zelda. "My sister dragged me here on false pretenses, all because I thought I saw our mother in my bathroom mirror three days ago."

"Ah Tabitha Wick," Yamgov reminisced. "Yes, I remember her well, a lovely woman, but yes, she was a person quite badly afflicted with ze crazy."

I couldn't quite place where Yamgov was from, but there was an eastern-bloc twang to his voice. "Is there anything you can tell us about her?" I asked. "Do you know why she went crazy and disappeared?"

"No one knows why she disappeared," Yamgov said placidly. "But I attributed her unpredictable mental state to her liking of practicing seriously powerful magic. Your mother was forever in Compass Cove's magical library, she was one of the only people in town with access to the magic books in the restricted section."

"Compass Cove has a magical library?" I asked. "...With a restricted section?"

Yamgov nodded. "Have you not taken your sister to the library yet, Zelda Wick?"

Zelda shuffled in her chair, like a child being admonished by a teacher. "In my defense things have been a little busy ever since Zora got here."

"Ah yes." Yamgov chuckled to himself and thumbed at a pile of newspapers stacked high on the corner of his desk. "I've seen you in there a few times. Keeping busy, eh Zora? They're calling you a great mystery solver."

"Look it's not like I'm trying to land myself in these situations, they just happen."

"Why did mom have access to the restricted section of the library?" Zelda asked.

Yamgov shrugged. "I don't know, I never asked her. In here things are strictly business. People that have access to the restricted section usually have a pretty good reason, and I don't think they're supposed to talk about it all that much. I think I do recall her talking about a research project once..." he said, staring up at the ceiling as he tried to remember.

"Is there any chance we could have a look at her medical records?" I asked. "Go through your notes and see if we can find anything useful?"

"I'm afraid not, no, not without the explicit permission of the patient, and as we all know…"

"Yeah, yeah, I get it," I said. Mom was missing, and had been missing for twenty years, so we weren't about to get permission from her anytime soon.

"Look if it's any consolation seeing your mother in the mirror is not that unusual," Yamgov said.

"It isn't?" Zelda and I both asked at the same time.

"Well, no!" Yamgov chuckled. "You are both the mirror image of your mother, I mean really it's uncanny!" he said. "Are you sure you weren't just looking at yourself?" Yamgov asked.

"My reflection doesn't run out of the mirror all that often," I said. "Or look terrified to see me. Besides, I have an Olaphax—" I saw Yamgov open his mouth to question. "A Time Owl, and she said my mom was in the bathroom, that's how I found her in the mirror!"

"Ah well…" Yamgov said, his smile fading a little as the appointment ended with uncertainty. "The results say you're *not* crazy, but I can always re-run the tests?"

Zelda made a sound that was a mix of snorting and laughter. Once again, I glared at her. "I think I'll take your word for it. Not crazy. Maybe you could sign a piece of paper. I'll laminate it and hang it around my neck, it will make my days a lot easier."

Zelda and I got up to go, Yamgov escorting us to the door of the office on our way out. "If I might make one more suggestion, perhaps it's worth your while visiting the library at some point? I believe the staff has hardly changed; they might be able to give you some more information on your mother."

"It's not a bad idea, thanks."

After saying goodbye at the door Zelda and I made our way back to the ground floor, following the maze of hallways and corridors. "That wasn't so bad," Zelda said cheerily. "Want to get some lunch?"

"After you just tried to commit me? No thanks, I'm going to head back home and get things ready for tomorrow morning. What have you got planned? Going to snitch on some school kids for not doing their homework? Film people jaywalking?"

"Very funny," Zelda said tonelessly. "I was just looking out for you, I'm concerned."

"Next time be more upfront, I don't want to get hoodwinked again."

"Alright that's fair, I'm sorry. But hey, Doctor Yamgov gave us a lead, didn't he? Why don't we check out the library this week?"

"I suppose you're right, which is a little annoying." I pouted. "We'll go to the library, but you'll have to make it up to me with donuts first."

"You own a bakery, just make some!"

"Nah, doesn't count. I want someone else to make them, what do you—argh!"

Zelda and I both screamed as we came into the abandoned lobby. We were just heading for the door when the translucent blue figure of my Aunt Constance floated upside down from the ceiling, a manic grin pressed upon her face.

We had routinely told her off about appearing out of nowhere and scaring us like this, but I was starting to suspect she enjoyed it. "Sorry, didn't mean to scare you!" she said cheerily.

"Why don't I believe that?" I realized Zelda and I were both holding each other tight, and I let go of her. "What do you want, Constance?"

"Just wanted to see how the doctor's appointment went. Also—BREAD WEEK!" she screamed.

Zelda and I both reared our heads back. "Why are you screaming?!" I asked.

"BREAD WEEK!" she hollered again. "We just got wind of it. It's happening, this week, bread week!"

"And bread week is…?" I asked, still lost.

"It's a bread fair with a competition," Zelda said casually. "Usually it revolves around complex bread sculpture. All local food businesses enter a piece, it's very good exposure. Celeste and I entered last time, didn't place though. There are several bread bakeries in town, and they obviously clean up. They only ever announce the fair at the last minute, kind of an odd tradition."

"Sounds about right for this town," I said. I looked at Constance. "Why are you so hype about it though?"

"It's a big deal, Zora! Massive chance to get more eyes on the bakery. And we need eyes, desperately!"

"I mean I don't know anything about bread, so…"

"So you better start baking! I'm thinking Statue of Liberty this year!" Constance shrieked as she flew out the door. She was shouting as she did so, her voice still audible even as she vanished into the distance. "BREAD WEEK!"

CHAPTER 2

Monday morning came around and I woke up early to get things ready for the bakery. I quite liked the frantic prep involved with getting the bakery ready for the day, I made everything from scratch and started fresh every morning—I wasn't taking any shortcuts with this stuff.

Since moving here to Compass Cove the bakery had been re-open for just over a month now, and during that short time it had been a rollercoaster of ups and downs. When we first opened people were lining up around the block, but since then the novelty had worn off, and the fact that I kept getting tangled in murder mysteries didn't help either.

Zelda and I had recently taken the mobile baking van out on the road to great success, but after a local gossip journalist put my face on the frontpage of the paper and accused me of murder business had pretty much dropped off a cliff.

The paper did have to run a story clearing my name however once I'd caught the real killer. People said there was no such thing as bad publicity… I think those people have never had their face plastered on the frontpage in a negative light.

Despite the ups and downs, business was starting to pick up again and that morning I did have a steady trickle of customers. What was even stranger is that they were all pleasant and easy to talk to! Since opening the bakery I'd learned that some members of the general public became different people when they stepped into a food service environment. Needless to say, I'd had my fair share of crazies in here, but they usually weren't in here for long. As I was the owner of this place, I could talk smack as much as I wanted, there was no 'customer is always right business here'. Come in here with a rude attitude, running your mouth? Hit the road baby!

As mid-morning came around a lull occurred, and it had been over half an hour since I'd seen a customer. As it was quiet, I went into the back and decided to practice some bread baking, just so I could appease Constance when she inevitably showed up. Even though this was a bakery I didn't have much in the way of bread. Cakes and sweets were my jam, and bread was a notoriously difficult beast, completely different to the type of baking I'd grown accustomed to since working here.

That said, bread didn't seem all that hard—in practice. Make a dough. Kneed that dough. Let it prove, possibly kneed it some more, possibly shape it, prove it again, bake it, voila!

After a little research I set to work on a simple loaf. I decided if I could get this right, I could try something fancier, like a plaited bread. Halfway through the process I slipped into a daydream and began talking to myself, pretending that I was being interviewed by Oprah.

"Why yes, when I started the first bakery it was hard! But after several years of hard work and graft, I got to where I am today. How many? We have six-hundred bakeries across the country now, that's right, the largest independent-owned baking franchise in the continental United States..." Pause for imaginary applause. "Would I say I'm a voice of a generation? I don't know I'd go that far but—"

"Who in the Dickens are you talking to?" Hermes said as he strolled into the kitchen.

For a moment I considered coming up with a lie—after all I'd been doing something rather embarrassing—but for some reason I just blurted out the truth instead. "Imaginary interview with Oprah."

"Ooh!" Hermes said, jumping up onto a chair that I had earlier deemed the appropriate cat sitting area in the kitchen. "I do those all the time. How did it go?"

"Oh, brilliantly. I was telling her all about my hugely successful bakery franchise. I'm obviously also a big philanthropist, and an award-winning novelist."

"Oh, of course," Hermes said astutely.

"What about you?" I asked.

"Me?" he queried.

"What do you talk about in your imaginary interviews?"

"Usually about my brimming career in film. Yeah, I'm the world's first A-list actor who is also a cat. I'm also a Rockstar."

I nodded my head to show I was impressed. "I always knew you could do it."

"Thanks, I actually mention you as a source of inspiration in my interviews. You've got to thank the little people, even when you hit the big time."

"I'm going to pretend I didn't hear the part where you call me 'little people'," I said, turning around to pull the bread out of the oven.

"What is that?" Hermes asked. "Some sort of cake?"

"This is bread, ever heard of it?" I said with a raised brow. I set the loaf down and released it from its tin. It came out fine, looked like it had risen well and smelled amazing.

"We do cakes here Zora, not bread!"

"Yeah, well Constance wants me to take part in some stupid bread week—"

"BREAD WEEK?!" he bellowed. "Is that this week?! This is bad, this is really bad!"

"I think everyone needs to calm down by a million percent. It's just some stupid bread fair, and I don't really care all that much about winning."

"*You* might not care, but I'd bet you care if you knew that Kaiser Klaus is going to be there, judging the entries!"

"...Who?"

Hermes opened his mouth and stared at me in disbelief. "Seriously? Kaiser Klaus? The bread king? The Beast from the Yeast? Old Daddy Dough Ba—"

"Let me stop you right there, I don't know who this guy is. Care to shed some light?"

"You seriously live under a rock. Don't you watch that Bread Wars show on tv? It's only the greatest. He's the main presenter on that. The guy knows his bread, and he's got a huge fanbase. Winning a local competition judged by Kaiser Klaus could put serious eyes on the shop! You know he's originally from Compass Cove?"

"But we're not really a bread place anyway, so it doesn't matter..."

"Plus I think there's some $10,000 prize as well," Hermes added as though it were an afterthought.

"Wait, $10,000?" I asked. "Constance mentioned nothing about that."

"That's because she's crazier than a bag of cats. To be honest though the money's just the cherry on the cake. The real prize of course is meeting Kaiser."

"Is it?" I asked in a high-pitched voice. "Still, you've renewed my interest, we could definitely do with a cash injection, and it's just bread, how hard could it be?" Hermes laughed heartily at the question. "What?!"

"I take it you haven't looked up the winners from the past few years. The competition is *fierce*. People come out in force to try and win this thing."

"Really?" I pulled my phone out and did a quick search for previous winners, after scrolling through photos of some amazing looking bread sculptures I put my phone back in my pocket and looked at my now-disappointing loaf. "On second though I'm not so sure I should even turn up at all."

"Oh, we're going girl!" Hermes brimmed with determination. "The whole town will be there anyway, it's not like there'll be anything else to do!"

There was a loud metallic knock then from the back door that led into the alleyway. I took my apron off and opened the door to find

Hudson. He looked pretty beat up and was holding one of his arms in a strange way.

"Hey!" he said cheerily. He smiled, and I saw that one of his front teeth was broken.

"Hudson? What the heck happened to you?"

"Tizzie-Whizzie," he said through a pained breath, like that explained anything. "Mind if I come in? My communicator got broken, I need to borrow a phone."

"Come in, come in," I urged him. Hudson limped his way inside and sat down at the kitchen island, grimacing as he did so. Hudson was a… friend of mine, a very attractive friend who was tall, dark and handsome.

When I first came to Compass Cove he was posing as an outlaw biker, but I since found out he was an agent for a secret magical organization. Hudson's job was to help take care of any rogue magical business that cropped up in human settlements, and apparently Compass Cove was rife for that kind of thing. Although he was only human and not magical, it appeared that Hudson had been magically enhanced in several ways, because his speed and strength was pretty much supernatural—for example I'd seen the guy fight a werewolf, and he'd held his own just fine.

"Marmalade on a mackerel!" Hermes exclaimed as he saw Hudson. "You look like you got thrown into an industrial tumble dryer with some bricks!"

"Yeah, I pretty much feel that way too." Hudson laughed, thanking me as I handed him an icepack. "I was trying to capture a Tizzie-Whizzie that's ventured too close to town. Little sucker is a particularly vicious one."

Hermes sucked air through his teeth like he only knew too well. "Well that's me not going outside until that thing is gone. I've heard the horror stories!"

"I'm sorry, what's a *'Tizzie-Whizzie'*, is the town in some sort of mortal danger?" I asked.

Hudson shook his head.

"It's a magical animal, sort of looks like a small hedgehog with wings."

I blinked, staring at Hudson for a moment. "I'm sorry, you're saying that a winged hedgehog did this to you?"

"Don't be deceived, Zora, the Tizzie-Whizzie is a Category 3 magical problem in MAGE's eyes. They're relatively harmless until you try to get them to leave an area. Humans can't see them, only magic folk."

"So why not let it hang around until it leaves?"

"Because those buggers get through food like it's going out of fashion. Two weeks unchecked and that lone Tizzie-Whizzie will work its way through every damn cupboard in this town."

"...I still don't understand how a little winged hedgehog beat you up so bad. I've seen you fight much worse!" I had to look up a picture on my phone just to be sure Hudson's definition of little didn't actually mean 'horse-sized'. Sure enough I was looking at pictures of little winged hedgehogs.

"Don't be fooled by their appearance, they are extremely fast and extremely strong. They have the fastest metabolism of any creature on the planet, that's why they eat so much food. I made the mistake of trying to tranquilize the little guy but I missed. I've just spent the last twenty minutes being thrown across the rooftops of town while that thing beat the crap out of me."

I tried to picture it in my mind, but I just couldn't see it. Hudson, a giant of a man, against a little winged hedgehog?

"Can I help?"

"No," he said quickly. "I don't want you to get involved. MAGE specifically put me here to make sure dangerous things like this don't cross your path. Once the Tizzie-Whizzie puts you on its bad list you're there for life."

"It's such a cute name though...and it's a hedgehog..." My attention moved to Hudson's arm, which only now did I realize was at an angle that didn't look right. "Is your arm broken?"

"Yeah, some of my ribs too I think. Normally I can portal back to MAGE HQ for a patch up, but—" Hudson let his broken arm flop on the table and with his other hand he pulled out a crushed electronic device. "Damaged in the fight. These things are designed to survive a nuclear blast."

"But it's a winged hedgehog…" I said once more, still wondering how such a small creature could cause so much damage. I snapped myself out of it. "I'll go and get you the phone from upstairs, be right back." A minute later I sprinted back down and handed the flamingo phone to Hudson, who had—somehow—ripped off his shirt and made himself a sling in my short absence from the room.

"Here you—oh," I said, handing him the phone and trying not to stare at his bare chest. It was covered in scratches and large bruises. This little winged hedgehog really *had* done a number on him.

Hudson made a quick call to MAGE and once he was done handed the phone back. "They'll be here to pick me up in five minutes. Thanks for helping me out, Zora, I appreciate it. I lost the little runt a few streets over and then I ran to the closest safe place I could think of. It wasn't following me, I made sure of that. I think it got bored of throwing me around."

"It's okay, don't mention it. Do you want some bread? I'm practicing for my 8th place finish at the bread fair this week."

"8th?" Hermes laughed. "Optimistic."

"The bread smells amazing, I'll have some, thanks."

I cut Hudson a slice and buttered it, he took a bite and a faint glow passed through his body. His arm was still broken, and he still looked like he'd had the crap kicked out of him, but he looked a little better.

"Hmm, that's the stuff," he savored, swallowing down the last bite. "There magic in this?"

"Somewhat, it's part of the outcome. The food of a kitchen witch nourishes whoever eats it, healing them in whatever way they need. Although I think you'll need more than one slice of bread for this."

He laughed in agreement. "I think you're right. Still, it's taken the pain away. Thank you."

Just as Hudson was leaving my cousin Sabrina showed up. She was the tallest out of all the girls in the family, and somehow managed to always look amazing no matter what she was wearing. It was kind of irritating to be honest, but she was still my girl.

Sabrina did a double take when she passed Hudson. "Woah, hello!" she remarked, taking a second to let her eyes linger on his beat-up body. Her eyes wide with tantalization she looked at me. "Are you going to introduce me to your bruised friend, Zora?"

Although Sabrina and Hudson hadn't yet met, Sabrina knew full well that this was Hudson. My cousins were obsessed with the potential romantic threads of my life, even though Hudson was nothing more than a friend. "Sabrina this is Hudson. Hudson this is my cousin, Sabrina."

"Nice to meet you," Hudson said cordially.

"Likewise... were you in a car accident or something?" she asked, not even hiding the fact that she was staring at his body now.

"There's a Tizzie-Whizzie on the loose," he said.

"A what now?"

"Small, winged hedgehog," I recapped. "Apparently, they're bad news. Who knew?"

A beep echoed from down the alleyway. "That's my ride, I best get going. Thanks again Zora." Hudson shuffled out of the doorway and out of sight, Sabrina making sure to milk the view for as long as she could. Once she looked back at me and saw my reproachful look her dreamy smile dropped from her face. "What?! A girl can look!"

"Are you coming in?" I asked, wondering what she was doing here.

"Actually I was hoping you could come somewhere with me, if you're not too busy."

I yanked my thumb in the direction of the bakery behind me. "Kind of running a business here bro."

"I know, I know. Maybe you could close for twenty minutes while we check this thing out? It's kind of urgent. I think it involves dark witches."

My heart caught in my throat. "Wait a second, did you say dark witches?" Sabrina nodded. I stared at my cousin cautiously for a moment then. A troupe of dark witches that called themselves the Sisters of the Shade had tried to attack me recently and lured me to a dangerous location by imitating my cousin Sabrina's voice.

Obviously Sabrina had nothing to do with it, but this felt strangely reminiscent, and my guard had been up ever since that first attack. I was being paranoid, but I wondered if perhaps this was another trick, was this even my real cousin?

"Zora? Are you there? Why are you looking at me like that?" Sabrina asked.

"Sorry, I'm just thinking about my last run in with dark witches. Last time they imitated your voice to lure me somewhere, and—"

"And you're wondering if I'm actually the real Sabrina, got it," she said. "Well you know there are magical spells that prevent the Sisters of the Shade from entering the town, so I don't think this has anything to do with them."

"You're saying there are other dark witches out there, and they *can* get in?" I asked.

"Uh, yeah," Sabrina said, almost making me feel like that should have been obvious. "Look Zora, the spells protecting this town are pretty comprehensive, but we can't keep *everything* out, it's just not possible! We're witches, but we're not omniscient, we don't know everything." As an afterthought she added. "Don't let Celeste know I said that."

"So what's the problem?" I asked.

"I was walking over here to come and say hi when I passed a brand-new bread shop."

"Oh, cool!" I said, but the look on Sabrina's face suggested it was anything but. "Or… not cool?"

"Zora that shop *wasn't* there yesterday, and then it just pops up today like it's always been around, something about it is giving me a bad vibe. Plus I'm pretty sure I spotted some voodoo insignia on the outside of the shop."

"Voodoo?" I asked. "Like dark African magic?"

She shrugged. "I don't know, but I think we should go and check it out. What do you think?"

I looked back at Hermes, who had somehow fallen asleep sitting up. "Okay, I'll give you twenty minutes, but no more than that!"

Sabrina grinned. "Let's do this!"

CHAPTER 3

I stuck a note to the shop window letting customers know I'd be back in 20 minutes, locked up, and followed Sabrina to the sidewalk.

"So how's your day going, apart from this evil bread shop thing?" I asked her as we walked along.

"Oh, pretty normal. No half-naked men showing up at my place of work," she said, giving me a suggestive look. "Celeste says you have *two* of these hunks following you around now."

"Feel free to take one if you want, they do my head in most of the time."

Somehow in my short time here I'd acquired two men that had deemed themselves as my 'protectors'. The first was Hudson, who worked for the secret magic organization, MAGE, and the second was Blake, a werewolf who was now working for the local police so he could stay close to me at all times.

Apparently, my ancestors had helped Blake's ancestors once upon a time, and ever since then they'd taken an oath to protect the Head Witch in Compass Cove. I wasn't actually the head witch in Compass Cove, but I *was* apparently a Prismatic Witch, a rare type of witch that could interact with all magic types and usually ended up being more powerful, so I'd been assigned a protector all the same.

"I might just have to take you up on that offer," Sabrina said with an eager smile.

"How is your love life anyway?" I asked her. Although Zelda and I had a lot of time to talk I wasn't with Sabrina as much, so she was still a bit of an enigma to me.

"What's the word, non-existent? I mean guys offer me their number every now and then, but I've been really busy getting the business off the ground these last couple years. I just don't have time to look after a man as well."

I laughed. "That's a great way of putting it."

"How's your magic going by the way? We'll have to go over a few more things before you start Magic School!"

Very recently I'd received a letter in the mail telling me that I'd successfully gotten into Compass Cove's Community School of Magic. Term started in a few weeks and my class would be in the evening. "I'm mostly just going by intuition at the moment and using those few things that you taught me."

"Wand holding up okay?" she asked. I'd gotten my wand from Sabrina's wand shop, and that was actually the place we discovered I was a Prismatic Witch, a witch that had the ability to excel in various areas of magic as opposed to one.

"No complaints so far, she's a beauty. To be honest I try not to get it out too much, I'm terrified of breaking the thing."

Sabrina laughed. "Yeah, I was like that when I first got mine. Don't stress about it too much, if it does break it's not the end of the world, we can always make another wand—one piece of wood doesn't define you."

"Wait, you make the wands?" I asked. I'd been in Sabrina's shop, *Wytch's Bazaar,* a wonderfully cluttered place with oddities around every corner. The day I went over to her shop to find a wand there had been hundreds of little black boxes everywhere.

"Yeah," she said with a laugh. "You're looking at Compass Cove's only certified Wand Smith. Where did you think the wands come from, you think they just appear?"

I shrugged. "I guess I hadn't actually thought about it. Maybe I thought they came from China or something."

Sabrina threw her head back with another laugh. "No, but I do get some of my Divination Wands from there actually. There are a lot of Divination Witches in China, they're kind of the experts."

"So, what is a Wand Smith?" I asked. "Like… how do you make a wand?"

"I'll show you some time!" Sabrina said excitedly. "I guess I never showed you the workshop when I gave you the tour of my place, it's in the basement. Some of them I make by hand, but wands made in a wand-lathe are stronger and last longer. They're quite difficult to use, and dangerous too, so not a lot of witches learn how to use them."

"Wand-lathe?" I asked in amusement. "I had no idea such a thing existed."

"Oh, for sure! I use an old steam-powered Gatorax-370, she's a real beauty. I could upgrade to one of the fancier La Zorca machines—all the Wand Smiths on the Witchgram love showing off its fancy paint job and sleek corners… stupid thing almost runs silent as well," Sabrina muttered.

"But you prefer your old-fashioned machine?" I asked.

"Huh?" Sabrina snapped herself from whatever rant was going on in her head. "Oh, yeah. I love my old Gatorax. Come over to the shop some time and I'll show you!"

"Sounds great," I grinned. "I will. By the way, what's Witchgram?"

Sabrina's mouth opened in shock. "Didn't Zelda tell you anything?!"

Just then I noticed a police car pull over just a few feet ahead of us. I saw who was behind the wheel and groaned. "Oh no," I said.

"What?" Sabrina's eyes saw the car too and they lit up. "Ooh, is this the other one? The dreamy werewolf cop?!"

"Yeah," I muttered, "And he can probably hear you."

Blake got out of the car and nodded at me, he closed the door and came on over. "Ladies."

"Officer!" Sabrina said, a little too keenly.

"Zora," Blake said to me. He was a mountain of a man, with long wavy hair, piercing eyes and a jaw that could break a bear's paw.

"Following me again?" I asked.

"Oh, only always. But you know that's kind of my job," he pointed out.

I nodded at the shiny police badge on his chest. "I thought that was your job?"

"This is just a cover, protecting you is the numero uno priority." He looked over at Sabrina. "Who do we have here?"

"Sabrina!" She said, practically blurting the word out. "I'm Sabrina's cousin. I mean, Zora's my cousin! Well she's my cousin as well of course but—"

"Officer Blake," he said, cutting off Sabrina's embarrassing stream of bumbling words and awkward laughter. Looking over I saw she was twirling her hair in her fingers.

"So is there a reason for the call?" I asked, prompting Blake to move this thing along.

"Yeah, it just so happens there is. I noticed that magical freak leaving your property this morning. Looked like he picked a fight with the wrong guy." Blake said the words with a satisfied smirk. He and Hudson didn't try and hide the fact that they hated each other. They were both bonehead alpha males that had essentially been assigned the same task—to look after me—so there was a lot of animosity between the pair.

"Uh yeah, something about a Tizzie-Whizzie," I recalled. "It's this small winged-hedgehog that he needs to get out of town."

Blake laughed and tried to suppress the reaction, poorly. "I'm sorry, a small flying hedgehog did that to him?"

"So he says."

"Well, I guess that settles it then—goes to show who the better protector really is. I bet I could get rid of that Tingy-Wingy no problem."

"Tizzie-Whizzie," I corrected. "I can pass you Hudson's number if you like and arrange a playdate? Maybe you could get rid of that thing together."

Blake shook his head in his arrogant way. "No need. I'll track down this little fuzzball and remove it myself. It's some sort of magical threat, right? That means it needs to go."

"Did you really just show up to ask me about Hudson?" I asked.

"No actually, I heard you say something about dark witches. I need to know where you're both heading."

"Wait a second," Sabrina said. "You've been spying on us?!"

"You call it spying, I call it around-the-clock asset protection detail."

"Apparently this is just kind of my life now?" I said to Sabrina. "I'd just try and get used to it. Neither of them go away, and believe me… I've asked."

"Come on, spit it out," Blake said. "Dark witches, what's going on? I'm busy also trying to be a cop, so it's hard to try and catch all the details."

"It's nothing, Blake. A new bread shop opened up and we're going to check it out, that's all."

"Huh," he said. "So you don't feel like you're in danger?"

"Danger of never having a moment to myself again? Very much so," I said. Sabrina laughed.

"Very funny." Blake rolled his eyes and looked back at his cruiser. "I'll get going then. Don't be a stranger Zora."

"Something tells me you're going to make sure I won't be!" I said as Blake walked back to his car. Once he closed the door and pulled away Sabrina and I kept walking.

"So many feelings right now," Sabrina said. "Like he's *so* hot, and I think I kind of dig the stalking thing, but it would also annoy me as well…"

"Right, but imagine *two* different guys doing it, and then you can see how the headaches start. Seriously, if I could give them both away I would."

"Pretty good instincts from muscles though, he sensed that we're up to something potentially dangerous. Why did you lie to him?"

"Because Blake is a hammer and the whole world is a nail. He's about as subtle as a brick to the face, and I don't want to walk into this voodoo bread shop with a charging bull that has something to prove."

"...I hadn't thought of it that way actually. The shop's just up here, come on!"

We crossed the street and I followed Sabrina down an alleyway that connected two different streets. It wasn't your usual alley filled with large dumpsters and steam vents, there were several business units here nestled into the sides of the buildings, and the one Sabrina led me to was halfway along the alley on the left-hand side.

We stopped outside a shop front with a large glass window. Everything was painted black, with accents of red here and there. The large sign over the shop read, 'Voodoo Bread', and there were strange symbols and drawings of skulls. The letters on the sign looked like they had been carved by and angry knife, all splintered and messy.

The large glass window was dusty and cluttered with strange dark trinkets. Inside I saw a dark and dim interior—this place didn't look like a bakery at all. I took a look at the faded paint on the shop's exterior and glanced at Sabrina. "This place looks like it's been here for years."

"Yeah, that's the thing though, it's not. It wasn't even here yesterday! Something weird is going on, I can feel it."

The mention of feeling made me realize my fingertips were crackling with magical energy. There was no denying it, something magical was going on in this place. Suddenly I felt quite nervous, I tried to swallow down my nerves and looked at Sabrina. "Let's... go inside then. Haven't got all day!"

We stepped inside the dark bakery, and Sabrina closed the door. Inside it was oppressively quiet, and the air felt heavy. Sabrina leaned in close and whispered, "Is that a snake?!"

Sure enough in a tank on the back wall there was a large black python, slithering around and generally just freaking me out.

I approached the glass counter to get a closer look at the bread on display and pulled my head back in disgust. "It's all moldy!" I whispered.

"What?!" Sabrina responded in a hushed and panicked manner. "We should get out of here before—"

A hand cut through a bead partition on a doorframe behind the counter. A dark-skinned woman dressed all in black slid into view, moving in a manner that reminded me more of a snake than a woman.

"Welcome," she said with a strong African accent. She spoke quick and to the point. "How may I help you?"

"Uh… uh…" Sabrina stammered.

"Uh… We came in here looking for some bread!" I put on my best smile, determined to try and appear friendly. I looked back at the rotting bread in the display cabinet and then back at the woman again, more than aware that my smile was beginning to waver.

"I'm afraid all our wares today are past their best—I wouldn't recommend it."

"Right…" I said. "Just… didn't you open today?"

"That's correct, Miss…"

"Wick, Zora Wick."

"Uh, Sabrina Wick," Sabrina offered as the strange woman turned her eyes on her.

"My name is Mistress Bridgette. I understand that this might look confusing today, but I assure you there is a method to my madness. Something tells me though that you didn't come here to look at bread."

I looked at Sabrina, expecting her to take the lead on this one. She was the reason we were here after all. Sabrina coughed and cleared throat. "Look it's just, walking past here I kind of got a weird vibe, and I can't help but notice the Voodoo symbols on your sign, and I'm—"

"You're worried that a dark witch has moved into town," Mistress Bridgette said.

"Yes!" Sabrina said, and then levelled back her tone to try and sound more casual. "I mean… *yes.*"

Bridgette smiled slightly, a dark glint twinkling in her black eyes. "You know Voodoo gets a bad rep, and understandably so. There are a lot of humans out there running around doing bad things, blaming it all on the Voodoo. The truth is that real Voodoo is white magic."

Both Sabrina and I looked around the creepy looking bakery. "No offense, but that's not really the vibe you're giving off," I said.

"Intentionally so." Bridgette smirked. "I'm a witch first and a businesswoman second, Miss Zora. Any good business has a strong identity and runs with it. The humans will eat this stuff up."

"Hopefully not literally," Sabrina said as she eyed the rotting wares.

"What's with the moldy bread?" I asked Bridgette.

"Voodoo is very simple. When things die, they release power. Voodoo is the process of capturing that power. I opened my shop today with food that is dying. It will grant great power and ensure the longevity of my new venture."

"Right..." I said. I suppose in a twisted sort of way it possibly made sense? "I guess I'll have to take your word for it."

"You don't have to take my word at all, come back tomorrow and you'll see—they'll be lining up around the block." Just then a look came over Mistress Bridgette's face, I couldn't be sure if I'd imagined it, but it was a look of maligned evil. "I guarantee it."

Shortly after that Sabrina and I made our excuses and got the heck out of the cursed bread shop, only once we were safely back on the sidewalk and several hundred feet away did we start talking.

"That's the last time I follow you on a little adventure!" I hissed.

"I told you something was going on!" Sabrina flapped her arms wildly. "She's a dark witch alright, even if she says she isn't!"

"I think we're jumping the gun here, we can't just go around accusing people of being dark witches because they look different and have rotting bread in their shop. She did explain all that weird stuff, there was a reason for it."

"Yeah, and did you feel that chill when she 'guaranteed' people would be lining up around the block. What did that mean?!"

"I don't know, but yeah... I felt something weird then too."

Looking past the surface of Mistress Bridgette and her curious shop, I couldn't set aside the ominous feeling I got from her. She said she was a good witch, but if it looks like a duck and walks like a duck…

"I've got to get back to the shop," Sabrina said. "I'll see you later?"

"Yeah, that's if Mistress Bridgette doesn't get you," I joked. Sabrina's eyes went wide with fear.

"Don't make jokes! She's probably making little voodoo dolls of us both right now!"

I gulped. "Wait, that's a real thing?"

"I've gotta go, see you later!" Sabrina ran across the road and headed down the sidewalk in the opposite direction. I shouted after her, but she didn't reply.

"Wait, Sabrina, is that a real thing?!"

CHAPTER 4

The next morning started normally enough. I was curious to see if Miss Bridgette's shop would have a line around the block like she said it would, but I didn't have time to get away from my own work to check. Fortunately I didn't have to, because just after I opened I received a call from Sabrina.

"She was right!" Sabrina started the call.

"...Who?"

"That evil voodoo woman! I went down to her shop out of curiosity and there's a line of humans around the block! I've never seen a bakery so busy!"

"You're kidding me..." At that moment I was in the bakery kitchen adding some decorative touches to brownie slices. "Maybe I should leave some rotting bread in my shop."

"This is bad Zora; I think this woman is controlling these people somehow. Mistress Bridgette is bad news!"

"What if it's her voodoo magic, like she explained yesterday?"

"Pfft, like I'm buying that excuse! She knows that we are both witches, she knows we're onto her voodoo mischief, she thinks she can throw us off the scent with a couple little lies! Think again!"

"Well, what are we going to do about it?" I asked. "I mean... my intuition is telling me that something *is* off about this lady. You think we should look into her?"

"That's exactly what I'm suggesting. I think we need to sleuth around and find out what she's up to. I've been looking for a chance to spend some more time with my new cousin, and I think this might just be it!" Sabrina said.

"Alright, you know what, I think I'm with you on this one. There are several things that don't add up about this new voodoo bakery… we can check it out."

"Yes! Awesome sauce. I'll come over later and we can start sticking string to corkboard, or whatever it is you do when you solve a mystery."

I laughed. "See you later."

LATER, when I was closing the bakery for the day, I dusted the last of the flour off my hands and hung up my apron. I headed upstairs to my apartment and magicked up myself a cup of tea while I read a book.

"Text message," Phoebe said on my left. At a glance Phoebe was an owl with iridescent feathers. Her plumage shifted through all the colors of the rainbow—quite a sight to behold. She was a new addition to the apartment, I accidentally magicked her up when trying to make a clock for my magic school application.

She was an Olaphax, better known as a Time Owl to most people. Apparently these special creatures were rare, they had a broader perception of time and could see into the future, but most of the time they weren't allowed to share information to prevent regular old folk from changing things.

"Text message?" I asked, looking over at her in confusion.

"You're about to get a text message from Zelda, it's about Celeste."

Sure enough my phone buzzed on the coffee table, I picked it up to see a text message from Zelda.

Yo, Celeste just snuck into the back, she's upstairs! Let's corner her, quick! Get down here!

Our cousin Celeste had been avoiding us the last few days after getting married to an eccentric old fisherman called Gordo who had at least sixty years on her. As of yet we had no idea how this arrangement had come to pass, and Celeste was making it darned hard to find out.

"I was right, wasn't I?" Phoebe said, her bright yellow eyes watching me with intrigue.

"Huh? Oh, yes. Thankyou Phoebe. Any chance I could have the lottery numbers for tomorrow?"

Phoebe blinked and didn't show any sign of amusement. She was quite a serious character; I wasn't sure if Time Owls really understood humor. "I'm sorry, I can't divulge significant future events, it would—"

"Yeah, it's alright Phoebe, I know, it was just a joke," I said dismissively. "Anyway, I better skedaddle. Celeste is—" I paused as I put on my jacket. "Wait, why am I telling you this? You already know what I'm going to do."

"Red car, jump to the right," Phoebe said placidly.

"What?" I stared at her, waiting for a more elaborate answer before realizing there wouldn't be one. "Well… see you later!"

Determined to get answers out of Celeste, I ran down the stairs, out the back door and along the sidewalk in the direction of Celeste and Zelda's café. It was raining quite hard, but I didn't mind too much, it was only a minute down the block, and I—

Just then I saw a red car coming down the street. My thoughts instantly ventured back to Phoebe's parting words in the apartment. Red car, jump right. *But why?*

Before I could wrap my head around the message the red car ran right through a deep puddle, drenching me to the bone in cold water, I stopped dead in my tracks as the cold took away my breath. "You have to be kidding me!"

If only I'd jumped right.

A minute later I arrived at the café, dripping from head to toe. I walked through the front door and saw Zelda doing a weird dance around Celeste as she tried to stop her from her leaving.

"Oh, not you as well!" Celeste said as she saw me enter. She turned her fiery gaze on Zelda. "Did you tell her I was here?!"

"I knew you'd try and run out again, so I called for backup!" Zelda said triumphantly. "Help me corner her Zor—" Zelda turned around to actually look at me and saw that I was soaked through. "What on earth happened to you?"

"I ignored a warning from an owl that can see the future," I said, taking off my wet coat and throwing it on to the coat rack. It was the end of the day and there weren't any customers in the café now. Hopelessly cornered, Celeste had given up trying to escape, and Zelda was no longer doing her weird dance.

"Sicco Celer," Celeste muttered, pointing her wand at me and my coat. A wave of warmth passed through me, and I saw water leave my body as tendrils of rising steam. I was dry.

"I could kiss you!" I said, already feeling a lot happier.

"I wouldn't, you might get old fisherman cooties," Zelda joked.

"Knock it off." Celeste huffed and put her wand away. "Can I go now?"

"No!" Zelda shouted dramatically. "We need to know why you married that old fisherman, and we need to know now!"

"What can I say, he's got a great sense of humor," she lied.

I looked at Celeste and raised a brow. "Come on dude, we're just trying to figure out what's going on here. We know it's not a real marriage. What's the deal? Is he blackmailing you?"

Celeste laughed. "Gordo? No. He's a saint. Wouldn't hurt a fly. It was actually my suggestion."

"What?!" Zelda and I both said together.

Celeste looked around the otherwise empty café and let out a frustrated breath. She pulled out a chain that was around her neck, on the end of which was a stunning blue gem wrapped in floral strands of silver. "What's this?" she said.

"I don't know."

"Constance's necklace!" Zelda said. "Her most treasured item!"

"Yup, and I got it after she passed. It was one of mom's favorite items, I wear it all the time. Well, last New Year's Eve I was partying on the lake, big boat party, lots of people all dressed to the nines."

"I've always wanted to go to that..." Zelda muttered.

"I was talking to this guy who works in a jewelry shop and got around to showing him the necklace. Wouldn't you know I picked the perfect spot of showing it off right over the bow of the boat. Maybe it was the New Year's cheer working through me, but I accidentally dropped the necklace into the lake."

"Yikes," I grimaced.

"I didn't know you lost it!" Zelda said.

"Yeah. I didn't say anything to Sabrina or you because I didn't want mom finding out, I knew she'd be devastated. I found an ad in the paper. It turns out that Gordo doesn't just operate the water taxi, he used to be a search and rescue diver." I opened my mouth to question that, because Gordo infamously liked to tell stories. "I know, *I know*, but trust me, he's telling the truth on that one, he showed me the photographs."

"That guy legitimately might be the most interesting man in the world," I mused.

Celeste chuckled. "You don't even know the half of it. Anyway, Gordo found the necklace, and I told him I owed him one, big time! If he needed help with anything I'd be there. I bumped into him in town a few weeks ago and got talking, and realized he wasn't in a great spot —he needed help, so I gave it to him."

Zelda and I both stared at Celeste for an uncomfortable moment. "...By *marrying* him?" Zelda asked.

Celeste closed her eyes and let out another monumental sigh. "He's been claimed by a siren," she said.

"Okay..." I said slowly. "And what does that mean?"

"There are a group of sirens that live out on the lake, and apparently Gordo has known them for a long time. He's one of the only humans in Compass Cove that they trust, and they want to take him down to the depths of the lake and turn him into one of them."

"What the frig!" Zelda exclaimed.

"Yeah," Celeste said in acknowledgement. "Gordo obviously doesn't want to do that though; the poor guy was riddled with nerves. I looked into it a little bit and found out that a siren can't take someone if they're married, so... yeah... the rest is history."

"Just to be clear, we're talking about mermaids here?" I asked. Celeste nodded.

"Damn Celeste, I'm actually quite proud of you!" Zelda said. "You stepped up and took one for the team!"

"Do we know for certain there are mermaids in Compass Cove lake?" I asked, still fixating on that point. "This could just be another one of Gordo's tall tales."

"There are," Zelda and Celeste both said together.

"They're nasty too," Zelda added. "They don't usually show themselves to humans, but they have no problems being rude to witches. One bit my finger when I was little!"

"Yeah they're a weird bunch," Celeste said. "Anyway, that's why I married Gordo, and I avoided you guys because I knew you were going to make a big deal about this thing, but it's said and done now. It's not like I was going to get married for real anytime soon, so I figured there was no harm in helping an old guy out. The sirens won't take him to the depths now."

"But what about when you do want to get married to someone for real?" I asked.

Celeste shrugged. "I don't know, we'll probably have the whole siren thing figured out by then, or I'll never get married. I guess we'll see."

"Admirable as this is, I think we might have to address this siren issue…" I said. "This solution seems like a temporary band aid slapped on a leaking dam."

Zelda laughed. "Zora, if you take one piece of advice from me in this life… and that's asking a lot… don't mess with sirens, they aren't afraid of witches, even a boss babe witch like yourself."

"There's nothing else to be done. The problem is solved," Celeste said. "You don't need to worry about this one Zora, honestly."

"Not entirely convinced, but okay, I'll respect your decision to be left alone."

Celeste beamed. "Now there's something you don't hear in this family very often!" She let out a relieved breath. "You know I'm glad I actually got to get all that off my chest. I was getting tired of hiding from you guys."

"I don't know why you were so paranoid about it," Zelda said. "You make us out to be a group of stark-raving lunatics."

"You were literally dancing around like a gibbon five minutes ago to stop me from leaving here," Celeste pointed out.

"Well, when you put it that way anyone would sound crazy," Zelda grumbled.

"I guess I should call Sabrina and tell her about all this then," Celeste said. "She's been driving me crazy, leaving like sixty messages an hour."

"You have to admit this was all pretty intriguing," Zelda proffered. "I just don't understand why you'd hide this from your supportive soul sisters in the first place."

"Yeah, it's a real mystery," Celeste said sarcastically. "Right, I'm going to head over to Sabrina's place and talk to her."

"You walking?" I asked. Celeste looked out the window at the rain and shook her head. "Not likely, why?"

"There's this new voodoo bread shop that opened up on route, stay away from it," I advised.

"Well *now* I want to check it out. What's it all about?"

"We don't know yet, but Sabrina and I are looking into it. We think a dark witch might have possibly moved in." I explained our encounter with Mistress Bridgette, the rotting bread, the ominous feeling I got from her and how there was a line around the block this morning.

"Definitely sounds like some bad juju," Zelda said. "I wonder if her arrival has something to do with the bread fair, that can't be a coincidence!"

Celeste said her goodbyes and Zelda made a pot of tea, we made a little dinner from the café's leftovers: a red cabbage coleslaw, a goat cheese and lentil pie, and some braised tofu. It was delicious.

Even though Celeste and Zelda ran a regular café, they were making preparations for the upcoming bread competition too. Zelda took me into the back and showed me one of their practice entries, an intricately woven chariot completely made out of bread.

"What the heck?!" I said, chocking in amazement over my cup of tea. "This is amazing!"

"Eh, if we get top twenty Celeste will be happy," Zelda said.

"People really take this bread thing seriously huh?"

"Well yeah, if not for the money or the business exposure, that Kaiser Klaus guy is pretty dreamy."

Intrigue got the better of me and I looked the guy up on my phone. Kaiser Klaus was by no means a looker, he was short, fat, red-faced, balding, and had these stupidly over-sized glasses.

"Seriously?" I said. "He looks like a cave troll that fell asleep on a sunbed."

"It's the hands, and his forearms!" Zelda said dreamily. "He's a master baker, spent his life kneading bread. He's confidently arrogant, you know, but in an attractive way?"

Personally, I've never much fell for that particular trait. Zelda pulled out her own phone and showed me some videos of Kaiser Klaus from previous years. He was the type of judge that criticized everything relentlessly, obviously choosing the character of a bad guy that people loved to hate.

"I wonder what he's like in real life, when he's not playing king obnoxious."

"Oh no, that's him," Zelda said. "He doesn't come off well on video, but you'll understand when you meet him. He's strangely charismatic."

"To be honest I'm tempted to skip this entire thing altogether."

Constance chose that moment to pop her head through the floor and scare the life out of us once more. "Over my dead body you will!"

"Constance!" Zelda screamed in frustration. "For the love of—!"

CHAPTER 5

After berating Constance for scare-jumping us once again Zelda and I left the café and went back to my place. Shortly after that Sabrina showed up and we spent some time trying to dig up information on this mysterious Mistress Bridgette. We couldn't find any information about her on the web, and stranger still was the fact that the Compass Cove Council website made no mention of a new business opening in that unit.

"Something is definitely amiss!" Zelda said with a finger held high in the air. She had a deerstalker on her head, and a long pipe too which was currently blowing bubbles.

"Where did you get that nonsense?" I laughed at her confounding detective cosplay.

"I brought it with me. I thought if we're sleuthing then we need to start dressing like it."

Despite looking the part we made no advance on the mysterious voodoo bread shop that evening, and now that Celeste was no longer hiding from us she came over too and we ended up playing boardgames.

"Ah, ah, ah!" Hermes said halfway through a game of monopoly. His piece was about to go to jail and Sabrina was moving him over.

"What now?" Sabrina asked.

"You don't go to jail if the roll was a double. I rolled two threes, so no jail for me."

"That's not a rule," we all said together. I think we were starting to lose patience with Hermes, who had spent the majority of the game making up his own rules and amendments any time something bad happened to him. At first we'd believe him, naively so, after he claimed he was a 'Monopoly master', but we were slowly cottoning on.

"Yes it is! Look in the rule book!"

"It wasn't a rule three turns ago when I rolled double threes and landed in jail," Zelda pointed out.

"Well, that's different, you don't have any hotels yet. They provide indemnity." Hermes held the belief with such conviction I was almost persuaded to believe him.

"Vote to eject Hermes from the game, all ye in favor raise your hand and say aye," Zelda said. We all raised our hands and uttered the word in unison.

"Sacrilege!" Hermes said in mock outrage. "If I had thumbs I'd flip this table over right now!" He looked at me and smiled. "Zelda, can you flip the table over for me?"

"That's not going to happen, why don't you go and watch your shows? I think we're going to wrap this game up anyway." A long yawn escaped me. "Phoebe, what time is it?"

"It is twenty minutes after eleven," the time owl said in her soothing manner.

"What?!" Sabrina said. "Oh man, I better get home and get to bed, I didn't realize it was so late!"

One by one everyone went home, except Zelda who decided to crash on the couch. The next morning, I had to get things ready for the bakery so I was up a few hours before her. By the time she woke up I headed upstairs and made us a quick breakfast before she left.

"What are you up to today?" she asked over a yawn. "The usual nonsense?"

"Let's find out, shall we? Phoebe, what's on the schedule today?!"

"Ten interviews this morning for baking assistants. First one in five minutes. Jacob Sothersby."

I did a spit-take as I remembered *that* was today. "Oh, crepes on a cracker! I thought that was next week!"

"How are you going to run the shop and do back-to-back interviews?" Zelda asked.

"I don't know, is there a magic spell to clone myself?" I said, mostly joking.

"Yeah, but don't mess around with that sort of stuff. Those spells are dangerous. This guy in college once told me he had a friend who did a cloning spell and made three clones to help with his study load. Anyway one of the clones went mad and killed the guy and the other clones. Chopped them all up and pureed them in the blender and—"

"I'm going to stop you right there." I put down my slice of toast, my appetite mysteriously having vanished. "Is that a real story?"

"I think so, apparently one of the severed butts was talking as the clone shoved it into the blender, it kept screaming 'No! Don't blend me, I'm a butt!'" Zelda delivered that line with complete earnest.

"Do you think the friend that told you this story might have been pulling your leg a little?" I asked, framing the question politely as possible. Zelda tended to be a little naïve, a little gullible, a little wet behind the ears… a little bit of all the things that made me wonder if she'd spent the last twenty years living under a rock.

"Why would I let him pull my leg? I'm not going to let some random guy touch me!"

I just looked at my sister and sighed. "It's a good thing you're pretty."

"What's that supposed to mean?" She shook her head as I took her empty plate away. "Do you want me to help you with the bakery this morning?"

"Aren't you working in the café with Celeste?"

"Yeah, but she can cope by herself. I just end up getting in the way most of the time anyway. You look like you need the help."

"That would actually be great. If you run the register downstairs, I can interview applicants in the kitchen!"

"Bakery is supposed to open in two minutes," Phoebe said from her cage. "And your interviewee is two minutes away."

"Alright, you heard the magic owl," I said to Zelda. "Let's get cracking!"

* * *

"So, what kind of experience do you have in a bakery setting?" I said to Jacob from across the table.

"Heck, the deets are all there on the rez, babe," Jacob said. He was a young guy who looked like he had just finished college. To his credit he *was* wearing a suit to the interview, albeit with a backwards baseball cap, huge black shades and fluorescent pink sneakers.

"Yes, you're 'rez' is quite interesting," I said, turning over the single sheet of bright pink paper. "You like pink, huh?"

"It's my power color. Are you familiar with power colors?"

"I can't say I've had heard the term before, no."

"Everyone has a power color. Yours is probably yellow or some sort of stale brown shade. When you find your power color *seize* it. For example, you're probably wondering how much I bench."

"Not if you put me in a room for ten-thousand years would I have thought to ask you that question."

"On a good day, 140lbs, but with my power color?" He blew out air. "Sheesh, we're talking 145lbs easy."

"Wow, so..." I looked back at the bright pink paper in my hands. Jacob's resume was typed up in all caps, and though the presentation was a little unorthodox, it did look like he had several years of experience working in a professional bakery. "I was hoping you could perhaps expand a little. It says you're last role was at 'Little Mike's Rad Bagel Factory'. You said you were the head of production for two years, quite impressive, can you tell more about it?"

Jacob stood up, turned his seat around and sat down again. "First thing you need to know about me is that I'm very conceptual."

"Okay, can you expand on that?"

"I like to think of my resume like a dream board. The things on there haven't explicitly happened *per say,* but I write them down, imagine that they *did* happen and therefore I gain the experience."

I stared at him for a few long seconds. "I'm sorry, did you just say this is all made up?"

"No, not made up, *manifested.* I created a reality that I wanted. This time last week I was a high school graduate with no experience at all, now I've got six years of kitchen experience, all because I manifested it."

"Right... well at least you have your GED." I looked up from his resume after another moment. "Unless..."

"Yeah, I manifested that too," he said with an assured smile. "Look, I know what you're thinking, you're threatened that I'm going to swoop in here and take the business from under your nose. I imagine the board of directors *will* side with me at some point in the next few weeks and facilitate the hostile takeover, but I wouldn't take it personally. It's just business."

If we were in the desert a tumbleweed would have floated on past at that moment. "This is a small independent bakery... we don't have a board of directors."

"Well, that's business 101 right there," he said. "That's your first mistake. This is the kind of business insight you can expect to absorb if you bring me on board. Listen my father is *loaded;* we're talking big moolah here. Once I start, I can guarantee some venture capital will be coming your way."

"Are you bribing me to give you a job?" I couldn't help it, I outwardly laughed at this point.

"I'm just saying there are many perks to having Jacob Sothersby on your team."

"Couldn't your rich dad just give you a job?"

Jacob shook his head. "Nah, that's just what he wants. I'm sticking it to the man. Before this I was driving limos as a summer job, but it's just not enough of a creative outlet, you know? Don't get me wrong, I'm a killer driver, but I saw your ad in the paper and that was it. I knew my destiny was calling me."

"That's great and all, but I need someone with actual experience, and a resume that isn't made up—"

"Manifested," he corrected.

"Right, *manifested.*" I took a sip of my water. "Well, thanks for coming in Mr. Sothersby. I'll be sure to—"

"That's it?" Jacob said in surprise. "Aren't you going to ask me where I'll be in five years?"

It wasn't a question on my list, it always seemed a little pointless to me. As the next interview wasn't for fifteen more minutes, I decided it wouldn't hurt. "Uh sure, so where would you be?"

Jacob held his hands up dramatically as he gave the answer. "A lens flare comes over the screen as the international space station comes into view. In the twinkling void of darkness one stark white figure floats, detached from humanity and all hopes of survival. The camera cuts in closer to show me in an astronaut suit, calmly plotting a way out of certain death despite the surmounting odds. A voice comes over my communicator, it's Brad Pitt, who is voicing my CGI monkey companion—"

"I'm sorry, are you pitching a movie to me?" I interrupted.

"Yes, in five years my blockbusting sci-fi action trilogy will have taken the world by storm, in the third instalment we find our hero, Burt Laserdeath, trapped in the—"

"I'm sorry Jacob but we're out of time!" I said, standing up abruptly and holding out my hand to shake his. "Feel free to email me the rest of your answer. I very much look forward to hearing it, but I'm afraid I have another interview in five minutes."

Jacob looked a little surprised to have his answer cut short, but he tapped his head and winked at me as he made his way to the door. "I get it, you want it in writing so you can read over it more than once—I don't blame you, there are a *lot* of layers to my genius, so do I start next week or—"

"Just out that door in the back, we'll be in touch, thanks!" I said, closing the door behind Jacob. I came back into the kitchen and Zelda popped her head through the door that lead into the front.

"If you don't hire that guy, it'll be a crime against humanity. He was hilarious!"

"Unfortunately, I don't need someone hilarious, I need someone with experience, or the willingness to learn at the least. How's the front?"

"Good, I've been serving customers all morning, it's busy today!"

"That's good," I said. I'd managed to squirrel away a little bit of money since opening the bakery, but I'd need a slightly bigger cushion to comfortably take on someone else. Zelda ducked her head back through the door.

"Your next applicant is here!" she said.

I spent the rest of the morning in interviews. I'd like to say after the disastrous start with Jacob that things got better, but to be honest it was a whole lotta bad. The next applicant was a brawny woman from eastern Europe. She didn't speak much English and most of her answers followed the same format of a deep-voiced, "I smash it."

"Could you tell me how you'd prevent a souffle from collapsing?"

"I smash it."

"What would you do if you're supposed to open the shop, but you've lost the keys?"

"I smash it."

"How do you respond if a customer starts acting aggressively?"

"I smash it."

Admittedly I did give her a point for that last answer.

After that there were a couple of no-shows, a guy that tried to crack an egg and completely crushed it against the counter, a woman that had a weird amount of questions concerning workplace emotional support ferrets, and another guy that mostly seemed interested in my shoe size.

Fortunately, the last interview of the morning was with an applicant I found the most promising on paper. She was called Daphne, and I'd met her once before at another bakery in town. We'd got on straightaway and she had all the makings of a great employee. Her resume came through the other night, and I jumped off the couch with joy because I'd been secretly hoping she'd apply. On top of that

I'd had a vision a few weeks prior where I was shouting to a 'Daphne' in the back of the bakery, so it felt like it was kind of meant to be.

As Zelda ushered Daphne into the back I was worn out from the string of failed interviews. I already knew she was qualified, so as she came in, I offered her the job with my very first breath.

"It's yours," I said. "On the condition you don't ask me any questions about ferrets or the size of my feet."

Daphne laughed. "I know that look, it's the face of a woman that's been interviewing all morning. I used to work in recruitment... it would be funny if it wasn't so exhausting."

"Then you know the pain I'm going through right now. Do you have any questions about the job?"

"Ah..." Daphne sat down, she was dressed smartly, in a pink blouse and a long black skirt that went down to her calves. "When can I start?"

"Tomorrow sound good?" I asked.

"Yes!" she said, sounding keen. "I've been bored out of my tree ever since Marjorie's place shut down. "Do you have a bake book?"

"A what now?" I asked.

"Like a recipe book of all the current bakes and how you prepare them in the morning?"

"Oh... I do *not* have something like that. That sounds like a good idea though if I'm bringing other people on board."

"Yeah, it's kind of like an instruction manual for setting things up. Obviously, you wouldn't have needed one until now because it was just you. I need to learn your routine and ways though. I was thinking I could take it home tonight and study ahead of tomorrow morning."

I found myself just smiling at Daphne.

"Did I say something wrong?" she asked.

"On the contrary, you've said the only right thing I've heard this morning. I'll type something up today and send it over to you, though to be honest I'm happy to start fresh tomorrow."

"Awesome!"

"Did you have any bakes you wanted to bring into the shop?" I asked. "Any recipes?"

Daphne looked shocked. "Wait, you want my ideas?"

"Uh... yeah," I said, wondering why that was so baffling. "Didn't you get any input at Marjorie's place before it shut down?"

"No," Daphne said. "Marjorie ran a very tight operation, an operation that used way too much sugar. You mean I'd get to actually sell my own recipes?"

"Sure," I said. "From what I hear you're a competent baker, I'm looking forward to seeing what you can bring to the table. The menu needs spicing up a little!"

"I think I could cry!" Daphne said, almost seeming a little dazed.

"Feel free to let it out, just be aware we don't have emotional support ferrets. There is an annoying familiar upstairs though. By the way, are you any good at baking bread?"

"Not bad," Daphne answered. "Why do you ask?"

"This bread fair is coming up and my ghost aunt regards it highly. If we don't place in the top ten at least she'll be throwing frying pans at us for a week."

"Wait, I... what?" Daphne said, her forehead creasing with confusion.

"Ignore what I just said. This job is all perks, there are no crazy drawbacks! Do you think you could make me a Statue of Liberty sculpture out of plaited bread?"

"I uh... I think I could try?" Daphne said unsurely.

Standing up I shook Daphne's hand and grinned. "Then welcome aboard! You're officially my first hire! Oprah is going to love hearing about this!"

"What?" Daphne asked.

"Never mind. Thanks for stopping by, I'll get in touch with you later about tomorrow's start. This is going to be great; I can feel it in my bones!"

Nothing could bring me down now... right?

CHAPTER 6

The next few days went surprisingly well. Daphne was a brilliant addition to the bakery from her very first shift, and by the end of the first day it felt like she'd always been there. She'd brought several new recipes with her, all of which I loved, and she'd done several trial sculptures of a Statue of Liberty made completely from sculpted bread.

My Aunt Constance was a ghost and only the women in my family could see her, but after a little magical assistance from Hermes (I bribed him with a grilled cheese) he performed a quick spell so Daphne could see her too—it only made sense seeing as she was going to be hanging around.

"I should have hired you years ago!" Constance said triumphantly one evening as Daphne finished her fourth practice run of her sculptural bread masterpiece. "I always knew you were a good baker, how did I let that toad Slade hire you?"

"I don't think it's enough to win the competition though," Daphne said as she stood back to survey her masterpiece. "Kaiser Klaus is a stickler, and he can get really nasty when he wants to."

The Bread Fair, which had been looming over my head all week like the sword of Damocles, was taking place tomorrow, the populace of Compass Cove descending on the old town hall building, which apparently had a large convention room in the back. As the week drew on a fervent frenzy slowly bubbled to the surface in town, it was all I heard anyone talking about in the streets, and anyone and everyone with an oven was apparently going to submit a piece for the competition.

"The process is very simple," Zelda said later that night as she explained it all to me for the hundredth time. "Everyone and their mother is going to bring some sort of bread showstopper to the convention hall. Imagine tables and tables full of bread."

"I'm already in heaven—" I said.

"Klaus has a team of underlings that walk through the convention and take stock of all the entries. They have little notepads and write down the entrance numbers of bakes that look promising. In the end they make a shortlist of thirty breads, and they're the ones that go to stage."

Constance popped her head through the coffee table. "And that silky son of a gun has not once ever put us on the shortlist! Though I was never that good at bread to be fair. I can't blame Kaiser Klaus, he's harsh, but he knows what he's talking about... and not bad on the eye too."

"Are we talking about the same person here?" I said, pulling up a photo of the guy once again just to make sure I had it right. Kaiser Klaus was balding and short, with a ruddy face and comically large glasses.

"I mean that photo doesn't catch his good angle," Constance said defensively.

"There is *something* about him in real life," Zelda agreed. "I can't explain what."

I just stared at the pair of them in bafflement. "There *has* to be something in the drinking water in this town."

THE NEXT MORNING it was the day of the long-awaited Bread Fair. Constance woke me up nice and early by flying into my room and banging two pots together. "Rise and shine, rise and shine! We have to get baking!"

"I did set an alarm you know," I grumbled, staring at the ungodly hour on my nightstand clock.

"The early bird gets the worm, Zora!" Constance started banging her pots again. "And this year we're going to get that worm! I think a top ten finish isn't out of the question!"

"I think I'm looking up the number for an exorcist in the magic phonebook if you wake me up like that again." I threw the covers back, slapped my feet onto the floor and blew the hair out of my eyes.

Constance saw my deadly expression and sensed that she had perhaps crossed a line. She set the pots down gently and floated backwards out of the room, a wavering smile on her face. "I'll just go… do something somewhere else for a bit!"

Daphne arrived not long after that, fresh-faced and ready to tackle the challenge. She'd brought coffee with her, which instantly improved my mood by a hundred percent. We got to work baking the bread and prepping the workspace for her crafty sculpture work.

"You're so calm during all of this," I said, observing Daphne as she worked with a rock-steady hand. "I can't handle the pressure!"

"I *do* feel a little nervous, but I'm pretending this is just another practice run. I'm quite good at lying to myself like that."

The tactic paid off, because when the bread was all done and assembled properly the final sculpture looked terrific. All in all, it wasn't much taller than a chair back, but Daphne had somehow managed to work in an intricate amount of detail and the piece looked great from every angle.

"The bread even tastes amazing," I said, sampling one of the off cuts. Not only did we have to supply a sculptural bread piece, but a bowl of samples too.

"Now we just have the task of getting it across town without it falling over or getting damaged."

Fortunately enough we made the journey to the convention without any major disasters. Once inside we were given a number by the folks running the event and we placed it by our bake. We set it down on one of the many tables, there were dozens of rows, all slowly filling with dough creations of all kinds.

In the next hour the convention room was brimming with hundreds—if not thousands—of people, Daphne and I spent some time checking out the other entries (there were some really good ones… and some not so good ones) and also set up our stall in the area for small local food businesses to sell wares. Celeste and Zelda arrived shortly after us and set up too, their stall was right next to ours.

"Hold onto your pants ladies," Sabrina said as she swaggered in a little later that morning. She wasn't entering the competition, and didn't have a stall, but she'd come by to be supportive and also gorge on the food. "Word has it that Kaiser Klaus himself has just arrived, he's in the building, and his minions are starting the walk through."

Zelda, Celeste, and Daphne all let out an excited schoolgirl 'Ooh!' at Sabrina's news. For some reason it seemed that every woman around here had a strange infatuation with this bad-tempered goblin of a man. I legitimately felt like I was taking crazy pills.

"Are you all brain damaged?" I said. "For real? I just don't get it. He looks like a dwarven bus driver with an anger problem."

"His energy comes off much stronger in real life," Sabrina said. "You'll get it when you meet him."

Unfortunately, I didn't have to wait much longer for that to happen. The man himself entered the food hall not long after, a small entourage of brutish security guards around him. The crowd moved around and followed them with awe.

"He's here, he's here!" Celeste whispered excitedly. Looking around at my group of friends I saw that each of them was equally enamored at the sight of the tiny red-faced Klaus. He walked through a few stalls, sampling the wares for free—a look of disapproval on his face all the while—before he came in our direction.

"He's coming, he's coming!" Sabrina danced up and down on the spot, her voice a shrill whisper.

"Play it cool," Zelda hissed, "You're going to blow it."

"So, what do we have here?" Klaus said as he approached the stall.

He was looking directly at me. Now he was up close I could appreciate just how small he was, I looked down at his bald red head.

"I run a bakery in town, we sell sweet things. Cakes and tray bakes mostly."

"Don't like the sign," he said, disdainfully eyeing the sign on our pop-up stall. "Let's try something then. Give me your best bake. It's not bread, but I know a thing or two about sweet things." It was a joke, apparently, Klaus winked at the other girls and they all broke out in the most confounding laughter, loud and rapturous. I stared at them all in utter confusion.

"Uh, Daphne, how about a slice of your sticky toffee cake?" I looked back at Klaus. "Daphne is new at the bakery, and we've adopted some of her recipes. This is one of my new favorites."

Klaus took a toothpick sample of the cake and chewed a small piece of it thoughtfully. It had barely been in his mouth for two seconds when he spat it out into a napkin and wretched. "Awful," he said. "Too dry, too sweet, dreadful mouth feel." Klaus wiped his mouth and drank some water. "No disrespect to you girl, but have you ever baked before? Cat litter tastes better than that abomination. Next!"

Without another word Klaus carried on through the crowd to eviscerate his next unwitting target. The five of us all stood there for a moment with our mouths open, unable to believe he'd just reacted so horribly. I'd had the cake—it was none of the things he'd just said.

"Well, we can't disagree with an expert," Sabrina said.

"He *does* know his stuff," Celeste added. "Even if he was firm."

Daphne, who had tears brimming in her eyes, nodded for some reason as if she agreed with them. "It's my own fault. I'll make it better next time."

Zelda was still staring after Klaus, just shook her head and bit her lip. "God if I could find a man like that."

"Right," I said. "That settles it then. Something weird is going on here. No chance in hell you'd react like that if anyone else came in here and talked to us like that. Everyone in this town is weirdly infatuated with this angry little fart of a man, and I'm going to find out why."

"Don't rock the boat!" Zelda said. "The last thing we need is to get shortlisted and then kicked out because you're creeping through cupboards and sniffing coats!"

I just stared at Zelda. "What on earth are you talking about?"

"Zelda's right," Daphne said. "I appreciate the concern, Zora, but I'm fine, really. We know the bread is solid, so we'll focus on that. The day is still ours."

Reason apparently meant nothing in this strange cult of personality, so I picked up a sample of the sticky toffee cake and handed one to each of my friends. "Try it, all of you." They all did. "Thoughts?"

"It *is* amazing," Celeste said. "Good job, Daphne."

Sabrina chewed her sample slowly and nodded her approval through a mouthful of food. "Schgood."

I had to pull Zelda away from the sample board because after one bite she went straight into binge mode. "Just one more!"

"Save some for the locals." I pulled her away and stood between her and the stall. "Don't you guys see? The cake *is* amazing, that guy was lying, just to act above it all."

"He knows better than us though, Zora," Sabrina offered. "He is an expert after all."

The rest of the girls nodded blindly. "Yeah," Daphne agreed. "I guess we're just wrong."

"Will you listen to yourselves?" I threw my arms up in exasperation. I was done trying to reason with them, something was clearly going on here.

I decided to clear my head by taking a walk through the convention room by myself. I checked out some food from some of the stalls and tried to be anywhere that Kaiser Klaus and his fan group wasn't. I was waiting in line to get a drink from a vending machine when Constance came floating down the hall, doing backflips.

"We got shortlisted, we're in, we're in! They just announced it!"

"Whoopee doo," I said monotonously. "I really don't care; the man is a pit stain and he made Daphne cry."

"Don't you ruin this for me!" Constance said. "If one of his underlings hears you talking like that we could get kicked out!"

"Shall I go and tell him to his face then?" I grabbed my can of drink from the machine and decided to head back to my brainwashed friends. Another familiar face came stomping through the crowd then. It was Mistress Bridgette, the mysterious witch from the suspicious voodoo bread shop. She nearly walked right into me, and I had to swerve to avoid her.

"You?" I said. "What are you doing here?"

"I bake bread, don't I?" she said through her teeth. Her African accent was stronger now. "Last I checked this was a bread competition."

"Fair point…" I muttered, unable to help noticing that the mysterious voodoo woman was a lot angrier than the last time I'd seen her. "What has you so riled up? I'd be pretty happy after a week of round-the-block business."

"Business is fine," she spat. "It's that little idiot with the glasses that everyone is so pent up on worshipping."

I moved my drink away from my lips. "Wait, you see it too? I thought I was the only one!"

"Something funny is going on here!" she said. "Mark my words! That cretin just insulted my goat curry. Been in my family for generations it has, he said it was bland and derivative!"

"Yeah, he seems to enjoy insulting people, someone really needs to teach that guy a lesson," I said briefly recalling my own encounter with him.

A determined smile came over Mistress Bridgette then, her eyes wide in a crazy sort of way. "No matter, I know what I'm going to do. No one talks to me like that and gets away with it."

Suddenly feeling a little fearful, I considered Mistress Bridgette carefully. "…What are you doing to do?" I gulped.

A kind of mania had come over her. She leaned in close, the whites of her eyes shining like beacons of madness, a crisp white smile spread over her face. Mistress Bridgette dropped her voice to a whisper and uttered five short words in my ears before peeling away and pirouetting down the corridor.

"I'm going to kill him!"

CHAPTER 7

I got lost on the way back to the stall and found myself wandering down an empty side corridor that was separate from the main room, completely by myself. Realizing that I'd lost my way I turned on my heel only to stop in horror as I saw a man crawling out of the floral-patterned carpet.

Although I felt the crackle of magic on my fingers, I didn't need it to see that this guy was somehow magical, I mean how many normal people could emerge from the floor like some demon from the underworld?

"Can I… help you?" I asked as I watched him squeeze through a swirly bit of border between two roses.

"Just—need—a—minute!" he huffed, getting his waist through the narrow gap and finally clambering out onto the carpet to stand up properly. His face was red from the effort, and he was out of breath. "Bit of a tight fit!"

I stared at him; my brow furrowed heavily. "You just crawled out of a carpet."

The strange man chuckled lightly, as if it was an everyday occurrence. "Got to get in one way or another!"

"I used the door," I said.

"Apologies for the unconventional entrance. My name is Clarence, Clarence Hogman." Clarence held his hand out and I took it—for some reason. "I've been trying to reach out to you, but you're always surrounded by humans, so I decided to jump on this chance and introduce myself while I can!"

"Right..." I pulled my hand away and stared at Clarence. He was about the same height as me, but his suit would have fit a horse better. He had a large blue shirt, the collar extending over his suit's brown lapels. "So... what is this about?"

"Wand Insurance!" Clarence said, pulling out a pamphlet and thrusting it into my hand in the same breath. He had reminded me of an old-time snake oil salesman, and now I understood why. "Our records indicate you are now the registered owner of a wand—purchased from *'Wytch's Bazaar'*—several weeks ago! Now I normally move on things like this a little faster but me and the family have been on holiday in Antigua!"

"Fancy." Maybe I needed to get into the Wand Insurance business. "Good trip?"

"Oh, stunning!" Clarence said emphatically. "Blue waters, white sands. A paradise beyond compare! Don't go near those turtles though. Tried feeding some lettuce to one and it bit down hard. Sucker didn't let go for fifteen whole minutes, I was running up and down the beach, screaming like a banshee!"

"...Right," I said after an awkward moment. "Anyway, you said something about wand insurance?"

"Wand Insurance!" Clarence pulled out another pamphlet and thrust it into my hands again, meaning that I now had two. "Now I'm sure I don't have to be the first to tell you that you don't want to be caught without wand insurance. The wand is the backbone of any good witch and wizard, and they're pretty fragile things! Just the other day an old witch got trapped under a bookcase and died because she couldn't use her wand to free herself!"

"Would having wand insurance have changed that?"

"Oh, absolutely!" Clarence opened his briefcase—which I hadn't noticed up until now—and a miniature display table unfolded form it effortlessly, two large panels springing out in the same motion. On those panels were text and pictures outlying the benefits of having—you guessed it—Wand Insurance.

I glanced over my shoulder back down the empty corridor to make sure I wasn't going mad and looked again at Clarence and his pop-up presentation, which now took up the entire width of the corridor. I couldn't get past him even if I wanted to.

"When a witch has Wand Insurance and breaks her wand, ta-da!" Clarence picked up a demo wand that was on the table before him and snapped it. The wand glowed white and zapped itself back together. "Now if our old lady witch friend had insured her wand she could have moved that bookcase off her with ease and she'd still be alive!"

"I thought witches could do magic without wands?" From what I understood they weren't completely necessary, they just helped to make magic easier.

"You're a new witch, aren't you?" Clarence said in his salesman-like manner.

"Fairly recent, yes."

"You know how I can tell? Because you're asking all the right questions. Now the truth is that a witch *can* do magic without a wand, but if you—god forbid—find yourself in a life and death situation, a working wand might just be the thing that saves your life. Now we've got several monthly plans, with various protection options to make sure we cover every possible—"

Clarence began leafing through a large book detailing various insurance plans and turned so he was facing the same direction as me.

"Listen, Clarence, you seem like a great guy—I've never watched anyone crawl out of a carpet like that—" As I spoke, I started side-stepping away and squeezed around the wide presentation boards blocking the corridor. Clarence followed me, folding one of them out of his way.

"Wait, where are you doing? We didn't get you protected yet!"

"It's just—my cousin makes wands, so if anything happens to mine then I'll get her to make me another. Plus, I'm told my wand is a little rarer..." I paused, stopping myself from saying anything about my rare magical abilities. I'd been advised to try and keep my Prismatic Powers a secret—there was no telling if a magical stranger might be secretly aligned with the wrong crowd.

"We've got cover for exotic woods, and we even cover wands treated in alternative oils, I'm talking Geranium, Black Spruce, Blue Tansy—" Clarence counted on his fingers as he rattled off whatever it was he was talking about.

"Look, I've got a pamphlet, thanks. I'll call you if I'm interested. I've really got to go, a small annoying man is going to be insulting me soon, and unfortunately, I can't miss out."

Clarence stopped his chase, his bright demeanor shifting to one of sadness almost immediately. "Hey, you know what? It's fine. I'm just trying to help an honest witch out; I understand if you want to take the risks and be out there without the proper protection."

"It's nothing personal, I promise," I said, still backing away slowly, trying to end this agonizing interruption. I don't know how this guy had managed to make me feel guilty into trying to leave this unsolicited sales pitch.

"No, I completely understand," Clarence said indifferently. "You don't care if you're breaking the law, that's fine."

This time I was the one that stopped in my tracks. "What did you say?"

"What?" Clarence had already started packing away his pop-up presentation. "Oh, nothing. Well, just, you know, I guess the Advisory Laws of Wand Conduct laid down by the Wand Insurance Group don't mean anything."

"Advisory laws?" I repeated. "How can something be a law and be advisory?"

"It's a long story, but you should know that people *have* been arrested for not having Wand Insurance before, and it *can* happen to you."

As annoying as this guy was, I was starting to worry I was doing something wrong by not having this stupid Wand Insurance. "Look, I really am busy now. Can I call you back at another time or something? I'll sort this out, I promise, I've just opened a business, I don't want to go to jail. When does this need sorting by?"

Clarence looked at his watch and blew out air. "Well, it's already past due, but I might be able to sweet-talk the top brass back at HQ into giving you a day to think it over. If it's not sorted by the end of the week though they *will* send the Insurance Inquisitors out—and there's nothing I can do to stop that."

"Let's not get hasty here," I pleaded. I don't know what an Insurance Inquisitor was, but I didn't like the sound of it. "I'll get it sorted, I promise, you just caught me on a bad day."

"Hey, don't sweat it, I get it!" Clarence's down-trodden routine dissolved away, and once more he took on the mood of a light-hearted salesman. "Modern woman, taking charge. Meetings, greetings, it's a big world! Give me a call when you get five minutes, and we'll get this all sorted. It's quick, easy, and it'll give you peace of mind!"

With a firm nod I turned and walked away, looking back to see Clarence Hogman disappear by crawling back *into* the carpet. A few minutes later I successfully found my stall again in the food hall and let out a sigh of exasperation.

"I was starting to wonder where you went to," Daphne said. "Kaiser's doing the judging in five minutes, we've got seats near the front as we made the shortlist."

"I just got apprehended by a Wand Insurance salesman, he crawled out of the carpet."

Daphne laughed. "Oh dear, yes, they can be a little pushy, eh? I remember when I got my first wand as a teenager, a Wand Insurance Salesman crawled out of a paving crack right outside the shop!"

"So this is a normal thing then?" I asked. "I mean, normal for the magic world?"

"Oh yeah, just a part of life," Daphne said. "Best thing to do is just buy the insurance and then they leave you alone. That reminds me, I need to renew mine this month... Anyway, I'll be back in a minute; I need the bathroom before this judging starts!"

"Alright, I'll wait here and then we'll go together."

The food hall was considerably quieter now, it seemed that everyone had convened in the main convention room ready to witness the main event. I saw Zelda running back in my direction.

"Left my camera in the stall," she said as she ducked behind the pop-up counter. "Where have you been? You're going to miss everything!"

"It's a long story. Do I need Wand Insurance?"

"Yeah, you don't want to get caught without that. Didn't you sort it yet? You can get arrested, Zora! Come on, let's go!" she said as she hurried back to the main room.

"Can't, waiting for Daphne."

Almost as soon as Zelda left, I heard another voice behind me. "You're going to miss the show." I turned around and saw my cousin Sabrina. She was holding a footlong sandwich in her hands. Where she put all this food I had no idea.

"I'm going now, just waiting for Daphne. Why are you still here?"

"Technically I'm not part of the comp, so I don't get good seats. I figured I'd just watch from the door. You're not allowed to eat in the audience—stupid rule. Where have you been?"

"Do I need Wand Insurance?" I asked, cutting straight to the point.

Sabrina scoffed and shook her head. "Nah, huge scam. Never had it myself, though I've got like thirty backup wands, so I guess I'm a little biased."

"So I can't go to prison for not having it?"

She laughed yet again. "Nope, did they tell you that? That's a scare tactic they use to get idiots into buying their racket."

"But Zelda said—" I began, stopping myself as I heard the words out loud. "Yeah actually... that makes sense. He was just a sleazy salesman then."

"You got cornered by one? Sorry, I should have warned you about them—it completely slipped my mind."

Just then a large voice echoed over the speakers, announcing the imminent start of the judging. I saw Daphne running back over to us, flapping her arms with excitement. “It’s starting, it’s starting!” she said as she ran over. “Let’s hurry up before we miss it!”

“Wouldn’t be the worst thing in the world though, would it?” I muttered as I followed Daphne towards the front of the room.

CHAPTER 8

When Kaiser Klaus came onto the stage he was met with rapturous applause that carried on for well over a minute. All the while he walked around with his head held high, a self-satisfied smile stretched across his face. Very clearly his ego was drinking in this moment—he loved the attention.

Looking at my friends I saw they were into this just as much as the rest of the room, as I looked all around me, I saw the manic faces of a crowd going wild. You would think that a Rockstar had just walked onto the stage, not some Z-List bread judge.

This was largely a non-magical event, most of the folk in Compass Cove were regular old humans with a smattering of magical folk sprinkled in. There were other witches and wizards here today, yes, but by and large this was your normal run of the mill baking competition... that mysteriously had an entire town gripped in mass hysteria.

Kaiser Klaus himself was human as far as I could tell, the man had no discernible magical aura about him, but the way people acted around him really did have me wondering if something funny was going on behind the scenes. Being finalists we were sitting right on the front row, only a few feet away from the stage, so as Klaus came near, I stretched my fingertips out and for a moment I felt a very light crackle of magical energy.

Hm, maybe something is going on here?

After taking in an over-extended welcome Klaus put his hands into the air signaling the audience to settle down. The applause faded out into complete and obedient silence.

"Welcome to the 2022 Compass Cove Bread Fair," Kaiser Klaus said smugly. He looked out across the room like a king surveying his kingdom. "Without any further delay I think we should begin. It looks like we have an… interesting selection of entries on the shortlist this year, so let's get going, shall we?"

The format was simple enough, there was a long table on the stage behind Kaiser Klaus, upon which were the twenty breads that had made the shortlist from the approval of Kaiser's underlings. We had of course made the cut—though I very much didn't care anymore—and Zelda and Celeste's entry had made it into the final judging as well.

A cameraman was following Klaus around the stage and the video feed was projected in real-time to a big screen hanging overhead so folks at the back of the room could follow the proceedings.

"We shall start over on the right this year I believe," Klaus walked over to the table and stopped in front of an ornamental bread sculpture that looked like a lion. It was really quite beautiful. "Entry number 402," he said, turning back to the audience. "Come on up to the stage, who's responsible for this monstrosity?"

Two women from the other end of the front row climbed onto the stage and stood next to Klaus. They were flustered and visibly excited to be standing in his presence.

"Sally and Charlotte Banks," one of the women said with a nervous smile. "We're home bakers, it's a sage and onion dough with—"

"I'll be the judge of that," Klaus said as he took a sample of the bread and chewed it for a second before spitting it out. "Too much salt, shouldn't have made the shortlist at all. As for the sculpture work —" Klaus regarded the magnificent lion showstopper. "Did a toddler do this? It's… embarrassing! Back to your seats, next!"

The two women left the stage in floods of tears, babbling an unending stream of thanks as they did so.

"Did they seriously just thank him for being an arrogant whack job?" I whispered to Zelda. "That thing looks great! And I bet it tastes great too!"

"Shh!" Zelda hushed back. "Kaiser Klaus is talking again!"

After that Klaus carried on 'judging' the rest of the entries. He didn't have a good word to say about any of them and was relentlessly rude to every one of the contestants that came onto the stage. Mistress Bridgette had also made the cut apparently because she went up as Klaus reviewed her black charcoal python bread, which looked absolutely fantastic.

"Completely amateur," Klaus said with disinterest and spat the bread out into a napkin. "You call yourself a baker? This is embarrassing."

Mistress Bridgette just stood there, still with that manic glare in her eye that I had seen earlier. I was worried she was going to do something on stage. She'd told me she was going to kill Kaiser Klaus when we last spoke. Part of me thought she was joking, but now I wasn't so sure.

The dreadlocked woman snapped a finger in the air and sprinkled something onto the stage. "May you get what's coming to you," she said calmly through a huge, white-toothed grin. Without another word she left the stage, grabbed her bag and stormed out of the hall.

"Disqualified," Klaus said with little regard for the strange outburst. After Mistress Bridgette it was our turn to face the bloodbath. Daphne and I went up on stage. If It didn't mean to much so everyone else I would have already left by now.

"What do we have here?" Klaus said as he stopped to regard our entry, the bread sculpture of the Statue of Liberty. He looked down upon the fine work and smirked. "Trying to curry favor, are we? You know that my parents originally came from New York. Thought you could get some free points by playing to my sympathies?"

He looked at me as though waiting for some response. "Just put the bread in your mouth so you can spit it out already," I said through my teeth.

Klaus looked a little unsettled by my cold response. I was the only person in the room that could apparently talk to the man without worshipping the ground he walked upon. He sputtered a paltry comeback. "M—Maybe I will," he said, grabbing a sample of the bread.

To my surprise he swallowed the sample down and made a silent note upon his pad. "Not bad," he said and quickly added, "but not great either. Return to your seats."

"He loved it!" Daphne said with an excited whisper as we headed off the stage.

"Really? That's your take?"

After that Klaus breezed through the remaining breads and took a ten-minute recess to 'collect my thoughts, draw upon my incomparable experience and select a winner'. *Thirty minutes* after disappearing he finally came back onto the stage—once again met by stupendous applause—and addressed the audience after the noise settled down.

"First of all, I'd like to say this has probably been the most disappointing selection of entries we've ever had. Normally I place the entries one by one from 20th to 1st place, but this year I will only announce a winner—and let me make this very clear—by winner I mean that this selected bread is the *least bad*."

Another round of clapping erupted through the crowd. "Everyone in here has lost their minds," I muttered to myself.

"Before I announce the winner though, I'd like to disqualify another entry." Klaus walked right over to Daphne's entry and swatted it onto the ground. Daphne squealed with fright. "Boring, derivative, and plain uninspired," Klaus said. "Not fit for a dog, let alone this stage."

My fists were balled tight, my teeth clenched, and I was ready to spring forward and explode. Zelda sensed I was about to lose it, because she threw her arms across me and kept me in my place.

"Easy now!" she said in a whisper.

"You saw what he did! Are you going to defend that one?!" I hissed back.

"I have to admit it feels like he *might* have crossed a line," Zelda confessed. "Let's wait to see who the winner is, and we can leave."

Klaus announced the winner, a regular looking loaf made by a home baker named Gloria Donovan. Gloria took to the stage and wept her tears of joy. Klaus handed her a trophy and check and had one of his staff quickly usher her off stage so he could reclaim the limelight.

"Amongst this smorgasbord of disappointment one entry cut through the mediocrity. The bakers in this town have forgotten that above all taste is what matters the most, these elaborate sculptures and pageantry are a distraction—but they cannot substitute good baking. Congratulations to our winner... you almost deserved it. Farewell Compass Cove!"

After that Kaiser Klaus left the stage and disappeared into the back once more. Zelda and Celeste, who had made a bread sculpture of a sword and shield, were seemingly delighted with the outcome.

"He's right about the sculpture element," Celeste said. "We should have just focused on making a good loaf."

"Exactly," Zelda agreed mindlessly. All around us people were packing their things up and slowly starting to file out of the convention hall.

"Didn't the competition brief explicitly encourage sculptural elements?" I asked.

"Yes," Celeste said, "but I guess you have to read between the lines with Kaiser Klaus, I just don't think we're able to decipher and properly understand his genius."

"So this guy tells everyone to make a bread sculpture, then gets up on stage and chews everyone out for doing what he asked?" I shook my head as I talked, and something snapped in me. I jumped to my feet, my whole body shaking with rage.

"Zora, where are you going?!" Zelda said with alarm.

"I'm going to give this guy a piece of my mind!" I wailed as I stormed off in the direction of the backstage.

"Meet you back at the shop then!" I heard my friends call behind me. "We're leaving!"

A long side-corridor separated the main convention room from the backstage area, and in front of those doors two huge security guards stood dressed in tight black polo shirts and sunglasses.

"Ah, hold it right there," one of them said and held their hand up. "Where do you think you're going?"

"I want to talk to Kaiser Klaus," I demanded. "Let me through." These guys were massive, but I wasn't scared of their intimidation tactics—which at this point was mainly their sheer size.

"Sorry, but the competition is over, and all decisions are final. Mr. Klaus is packing up to leave, he's got another competition in Salt Lake City in three days' time. Now be on your way."

I was tempted to let the rage out right then and there on the security detail, but I thought better of it and turned around, marching back towards the main convention hall. The massive room was already half empty as the crowds filed out, but I noticed a bright blue spectral figure floating towards me—it was Constance.

"Wasn't it marvelous?!" she said. "Klaus was on top form as always. It's a shame we didn't win, but making the shortlist is victory enough in my eyes!"

"He pushed Daphne's entry onto the ground and disqualified us," I reminded her. "Am I the only one that can see this man is an insufferable arse?"

"It's called conviction, Zora darling! It's a rare thing these days to find a man that sticks to his principles!"

"Well, I think something fishy is going on here, and I want to speak with Klaus, woman to man! I'm trying to get backstage so I can give him a piece of my mind, but those trained apes of his are making it impossible!"

Constance made her ghost brows dance suggestively. "Zora! Never had you down for a groupie. If I was a little more corporeal, I must admit I'd be tempted too..."

"I'm not trying to hook up with him, you idiot, I want to put him in his place! Can you help me sneak around those guards somehow? He insulted your bakery by knocking our entry onto the ground!"

"On the one hand I don't want to enable this rebellious streak of yours, but on the other hand I've always delighted in mischief. I think if you speak to him one on one, *you'll* see he's not so bad, so I'm going to help you."

I stared at her and just shook my head in disbelief. "Unbelievable, but okay. How do I get past the guards? Can I use magic to control them?"

"Zora, mind control magic is the first step on a slippery slope towards dark magic, I wouldn't advise it," Constance said reproachfully.

"Invisibility? A disguise spell?"

"At your current abilities such spells all have unpleasant side effects. I think our best approach is a little spot of harmless prestidigitation."

"Presti—what now?" I asked.

"It's a very easy spell, a harmless sensory effect. You can trick other people into seeing things that aren't really there."

"Isn't that the same as mind control?"

"No, with a mind control spell you actively take control of someone's free will and make them move or act against their own wishes. Our aim here is to conjure up an illusion and trick someone into thinking they need to move."

"Ah, I see... so if I could make these guys think their butts are on fire..."

"They'd run for the door, exactly! It's very simple, hold your wand and focus on the area where you want the illusion to appear. Will it in your imagination and then watch what happens."

I pulled my wand from my magical aura and held it in a concealed manner so others couldn't see it. I took cover behind a vending machine and stared at both the guards before I willed the image of a fire into my mind. All of a sudden, I saw flames erupt from both of their rears.

"Fire!" one of them shouted.

"Fire!" the other joined in.

Both men immediately turned around, sprinted down the corridor, and disappeared from sight.

"And voila!" Constance said. "One door free of irritating security guards."

"That was amazing!" I said, marveling at the results. I hid my wand once more and sprinted down the corridor to the backstage area. "How long will they be out of my hair?"

"Oh, long enough to get in and out of here. No doubt they've plunged themselves into a toilet or something equally hilarious. A good illusion will usually last an hour, but that fire was surprisingly vivid. It might take them a while to realize it was all in their heads."

"Now it's just a matter of finding Klaus's dressing room," I muttered to myself as we walked.

"Sixth door on the right," Constance answered immediately. I stared at her in question. "What?" she shrugged. "I might have floated in there earlier to watch as he got changed."

"It's concerning how little interest ghosts have for privacy," I said. "But more concerning still is that people regard this man as some sort of sex symbol. He's revolting from the surface to the core."

Constance rolled her eyes. "A face-to-face chat and you'll change your mind, Zora, I promise."

I reached Kaiser Klaus's door and knocked on it. As I did so the door swung open in its frame, partly revealing the dressing room beyond. Constance and I looked at one another.

"Uh, hello?" I said. Nobody responded. Without hesitating I pushed the door open all the way and there he was lying face down on the ground, gagged, hands and feet tied, and a knife sticking in his back.

"Oh mercy!" Constance cried. "Who would take this angel from us?!"

Kaiser Klaus was dead.

CHAPTER 9

Despite being involved in two separate murder-mysteries since moving to Compass Cove I'd never actually stumbled over a dead body before. Needless to say, I was a little in shock. As soon as I saw the dead body I staggered back out of the room and shouted for help.

Klaus' entourage came running out of the woodwork and soon everyone was losing their minds, caught up in the chaos. Not much longer after that the police arrived on the scene, along with a face that was more familiar to me than others.

Blake came through the doors accompanied by Wayne and Zayne Combs, deputies and sons of Burt Combs, who was the sheriff of Compass Cove. The brothers immediately went into crowd control mode and secured the area while Blake walked over to me, his head turned with a curious expression.

"Trouble calls. Should have figured you were the one on the other end of the line," he said and stopped in front of me. We were outside the room containing the body. Blake's police shirt was pulled tight over his muscled frame, and he was wearing shades—he looked like an ego-tripping traffic cop.

"You know we're inside; you can take them off."

Blake muttered something about 'light-sensitive headaches' and quickly changed the conversation. "Where's the body?"

"In there," I said and pointed towards the door which someone had pulled partly shut out of respect. Blake took a large breath and steered himself towards the room. "Well, let's see what we have then."

Blake opened the door and took a few steps inside before crouching down and looking at the body for a few seconds. He stood up and looked back at me. "Quite the scene," he remarked.

"Yeah, someone bound his hands and feet, *and* stabbed him."

"I'm thinking burglary gone wrong," Blake said, swirling a toothpick around his mouth.

"Burglary?" I asked with uncertainty. "What makes you say that?"

"They tied him up so they could clear him out. This guy is some big time tv celebrity, right? He's probably got money."

"Yeah, but look around, the dressing room hasn't been trashed, and I'm willing to bet he's not been robbed. Besides, the attacker had a weapon, they didn't need rope to keep him obedient."

"That's a good point..." Blake mused slowly. "So why gag him and tie him up?"

"There's a lot of reasons. The killer could be sadistic, or it could be a precaution to stop him from running. Maybe the killer wanted to give them a piece of their mind before they finished him off."

"What were you doing back here?" Blake asked as an afterthought.

"I... came here to give him a piece of my mind." Blake raised a querying brow. "I *didn't* kill the guy," I said.

"I believe you, you're not stupid enough to go sticking knives in people. I take it this guy had his fair share of enemies then? Must have done something wrong to get you riled up."

"He wasn't exactly pleasant, let's put it that way. The strangest thing is that no-one else seemed bothered by it. This guy would insult people to their face, and they'd thank him for it."

"Well, that's weird," Blake said.

"Right? It's like I was the only one that could see it!"

"You think there's some sort of magical element involved?" Blake asked. "Maybe you're not affected because you're... you know," he lowered his voice. *"A Prismatic Witch."*

It hadn't actually crossed my mind up until now. Was it possible some sort of magic spell *was* at work here, and I had some heightened immunity because of my powers?

"Actually, one other person could see through it," I said. "This voodoo woman, she just opened up a bread shop in town. She's a mystery in herself, might be a dark witch."

"Voodoo?" Blake said, his ears perking up. "Think she can tie a knot?"

"What?"

"My cousin dabbled with voodoo one summer, more a hobby than anything serious. She made hundreds of little dolls from knotted twine, left them everywhere, it was pretty annoying. Those little dolls are called 'fetishes', it's a big part of the religion." Blake crouched down again and got a better look at the bindings on Kaiser Klaus's arms and legs.

"What are you saying?" I asked, not following his line of thought.

"I'm saying that I know my knots, and there are some unusually good knots on these bindings. If your voodoo woman makes twine dolls too then she could tie a knot like this." He stood up again. "Could she be a suspect? Did she say anything to make you suspicious?"

"Uh... yes actually. He insulted her cooking multiple times, she was livid. Said she was going to kill him."

Blake raised his brows. "I think we might be onto something then."

"In all fairness I felt like killing the man too." I quickly added, "Obviously I didn't. Also, I don't trust that woman, but she *did* storm out of the competition like an hour before I found Klaus dead."

"You saw her leave?"

"Yeah, everyone did, she didn't make a secret of it."

Blake's face twisted in thought as he considered the information. Just then his phone started ringing. "Hold on a second, it's Sheriff Burt." Blake answered the phone and put it on speaker. "Hey Burt, I'm here at the crime scene with Zora Wick."

"Howdy Zora!" Burt called. "How are you doing?"

"Tripping over dead bodies, but apart from that I'm not too bad."

"Mighty fine!" Burt said. "So, what do we have, Blake?"

"Homicide, victim tied up and stabbed in the back. No sign of a suspect."

"That so?" Burt mused down the line. "Well, I'll call Tamara and have her come take a look at the scene, see if she can find any of that science stuff to help us out."

"Tamara Banana? The town coroner?" I asked.

"You know her? She's our CSI."

"We've…met. I thought she was a coroner." I'd met Tamara recently during a clandestine meeting in a multi-story parking lot. She was afraid for her life, convinced the mob were going to put a hit out on her. Needless to say, everything worked out fine.

"Tamara's a swiss-army knife of usefulness," Burt said. "Now Blake, you still there?"

"I'm holding the phone, chief."

"Good. I want you to take this one. You've not had a real case since you started at the station, and I figure this is as good as any to cut your teeth on."

Blake looked surprised. "Uh, are you sure sir? I'm sure Wayne or Zayne would be better suited for something like this."

Burt sputtered with laughter. "Yeah, I'm not so sure. I know my boys and they never were ones for detective work. Besides, I need them back up on the coastal road with me—we've nearly finished shifting the debris from the landslide all those months back. They haul dirt better than anything else. You can work this one Blake, and feel free to take on Miss Wick as a consultant if you feel you need a helping hand—she's been a real help to the station since she moved here. If that's alright with you of course Miss Wick."

"I'll take it into consideration, thanks Burt."

Blake ended the call and let out a sigh. "Got to be honest I wasn't expecting Burt to put me on this one. I don't know the first thing about real detective work. You've got to help me out here."

"Dude I'm already busy enough as it is trying to run my business, I can't run around the town solving crimes every time someone gets killed!"

"Didn't you just take on an assistant?" he asked. "I'm sure you can spare a little more time now."

"How did you know—" I began, before I stopped myself. "You seriously need to stop this stalking thing, it's getting creepy."

"It's not stalking, I'm your keeper. It's my job to protect you, remember? All the better for you to work this case with me. If I have actual police work to do, I'll have less time to keep up surveillance and make sure you're safe. We work this together and you'll be right by my side the whole time."

"I'm sure you can handle this—"

"There's also the other angle you're not considering. People might think you're the one that did this."

"What?! People won't think that!"

"Are you sure? I can hear them whispering down the corridor. You *are* the one that found the body after all, and you weren't even supposed to be back here."

Great, this was all that I needed, being under suspicion of yet another murder. "Listen I can help you out *when* I have a minute, but I'm not going to be on this thing twenty-four-seven, I have a life. I'll need something from you before I agree to help though."

"Name your price, anything," Blake said.

"Take your shades off."

"...No can do. I already told you I've got light-sensitive—hey!"

I lurched forward and snatched the sunglasses off Blake's face, revealing two large black eyes. "I knew it! You were hiding this! What happened to you, have you been fighting with Hudson again?"

Blake snatched the sunglasses back off me and covered his eyes. "You think a pathetic little human like Hudson could leave a mark on me? He might be a magically enhanced freak, but I'm a werewolf, Zora, he can't hurt me."

"But something did, so what happened?" For a long moment Blake looked away and just stared at the wall. Then in a very quiet voice he mumbled something. "Speak up, I can't hear you!"

He let out a terse breath and looked at me. He spoke quietly and through his teeth. "It was the Tizzie-Whizzie."

I pulled my head back and had to hold back a laugh. "Wait, the little flying hedgehog thing did this to you? For real?"

"Don't make a big deal about it, it's already embarrassing enough! I went after that thing when you told me about it. Obviously, it's a magical threat that needs to be neutralized. I assumed it kicked Hudson's ass because he's a sissy, but..." Blake paused as he recollected something horrific. "That little thing is no joke."

"So we have a murderer running around and a winged-hedgehog is making short work of the two men meant to protect me." I couldn't help it; I broke out in laughter as I contemplated the ridiculousness of it all.

"It's not funny Zora, that thing has some sort of poison on its quills that stops magical healing. Do you know the last time I had a black eye? Never!"

"Alright, don't get your panties in a twist. Can't you and Hudson work together to take this thing down?"

Blake looked hugely offended by the idea. "If you think a professional like me is going to work with an idiot like him then you're crazy. It's already bad enough I have to run around town trying to clean up his mess. He's basically a magical animal control man, you think he'd have a handle on this."

"Maybe I'll just have to look into it myself then," I joked.

"No!" Blake said very firmly. "Zora I am not kidding. Do *not* go looking for that thing. It's deceptively dangerous. Promise me you'll stay away!"

I don't know why, but Blake freaking out over this only made me laugh more. "Chill out, I'll leave the magic hedgehog to you and Hudson. I've already got enough on my plate as it is—especially as I'm now apparently helping you out with this."

"Hey, we've already got a few clues—the killer was good with knots."

"Yeah and..." I walked closer to Kaiser's body and crouched to get a look at it myself.

"Don't touch anything," Blake warned.

"I'm not going to, don't worry, I just wanted to try something." I held my hands out and moved them through the air over the body.

"What are you doing?"

"I'm suspicious there's some sort of magic involved with this guy. I felt a very faint crackle of it when he was on stage."

"Is he a wizard?"

"No," I said and shook my head. "But people weren't acting right around him. It was almost like he—ah! There!" I stopped as my fingers picked up a faint crackling sensation around Kaiser's bound hands. Looking closer I realized he had a ring on one of his fingers. It was dark silver, almost black, with a blue gemstone. "I think this ring has magic."

Blake moved around the body to get a better look and confirmed my suspicions. "I've seen magic rings before. The markings on the band? That thing is magical. But what are its effects? Can you find out?"

"Me personally? No, but I might have a guy who can help. He's kind of an authority on all sorts of obscure magical knowledge. Only problem is that he's a little annoying."

"Hudson," Blake said.

"No, my familiar, Hermes. He's like a little encyclopedia of magic."

"Can you get him here discretely?" Blake asked.

"My Aunt Constance might be able to, where did she get to? Wait here, I'll try and find her."

When I'd first found the body Constance flew off, crying to herself about Klaus being 'taken before his time'. She'd headed back in the direction of the main convention room. As I came into the main room, I heard sobbing from somewhere above me and as I looked up, I saw Constance sitting cross-legged on the ceiling as she balled her ghostly eyes out.

Fortunately, the room was now empty, so I could talk to her without looking crazy. "Seriously?" I asked her. "He was a massive jerk! Get over it already!"

"Oh, go away!" she sobbed. "You don't know what it's like to lose a piece of your heart!"

She has completely lost her mind. "You need to stop crying and come down here. I need your help."

"Help!? You want my help?! I'm a mess Zora! Can't you see that!"

"Can you just fly back to the house and tell Hermes to come over here. I know he can do that portal thing now. Klaus has a magic ring on, and I want to see if Hermes can help identify it."

Constance just kept sobbing however, in fact I think she even got a bit louder. I didn't think she was *actually* that upset, but she liked to act dramatically whenever the opportunity presented itself.

"I don't think I can go on anymore, Zora. I might have to end things. I'm sorry you had to find out this way," she wailed.

"Things already did end for you. You're a ghost," I reminded her. That however did give me an idea. "And speaking of ghosts, won't you have a new friend soon?"

Constance momentarily paused her Oscar-winning efforts and looked at me. "What do you mean?"

"Well Kaiser Klaus will be a ghost soon, right? You can fly all over town with him for the rest of eternity."

Suddenly her face lit up, she flew down to the floor, a woman renewed. "My god, I hadn't even thought of it like that! You're exactly right, Zora!"

"Right? And if ghost Kaiser finds out that you helped solve his murder... you'd probably be best friends in the afterlife. Maybe even... more?"

Constance slapped herself in the face and looked me in the eye. "Right! What do you need me to do?"

"Fly home and tell Hermes to portal here. We need him to identify a ring."

"On it!" she said, and without another word she flew out of the room at breakneck speed.

"What is my life..." I muttered to myself and walked back to the room where Blake was waiting.

"Your guy coming?" he asked.

"My talking cat? Yeah, I think he's on his way. Should be here in a few minutes." With CSI on the way and an annoying cat that could identify this mysterious magical ring, we were beginning to chip away at this new mystery sitting before us.

I just couldn't believe I was going through all this once again.

CHAPTER 10

As Hermes could teleport, I assumed, naively so, that he would be over here in a flash. In actuality Tamara Banana, the town CSI, was the first to arrive on the scene. I didn't know much about Tamara other than the fact that she had a hilarious name. She came into the room with two huge suitcases that she pulled along on wheels behind her. Tamara was a petite and timid woman, with a head full of wild red curls.

"What do we have here then?" she huffed as she set the cases down. She made a look of recognition upon seeing my face. "Helping out again?"

"Apparently so," I said.

"Zora, right? Zora Wick?" she asked.

"That's right."

"Tamara Banana," she said, and we shook hands. "Just in case you forgot my name."

No danger there. "So you're the coroner *and* with CSI?" I asked, quite impressed at her wide-ranging abilities.

"I'm also the system admin. I should probably ask for a pay rise, right?" She looked at Blake. "Not seen you before, are you new too?"

"Blake Voss," Blake said and also shook her hand. "New recruit, Burt put me on the case with the assistance of Miss Wick here."

"Alrighty, well don't we make a fine little trio? Let me get the old rubber gloves out and see what clues I can dig up. Once we've got the science down y'all can get out there and shake down your suspects."

Tamara got to work investigating the scene. I stood and watched silently with great interest as she worked, while Blake was apparently more of a 'ask questions every five seconds' type of guy.

"What are you doing now?" he asked for the dozenth time. Tamara, who had the patience of a saint up until now, stood up and turned around.

"Alright, outside, both of you. This crime scene is mine for the next half hour."

"I didn't say anything!" I pleaded.

"No, but I work better when I'm alone, so get going both of you. I'll radio when I'm done."

"What's her problem?" Blake muttered obliviously as we headed into the main convention room.

"It's a complete mystery," I said sarcastically. "Do you want to get a coffee or something while we wait for her to finish?"

Blake stopped and smiled at me. "Are you asking me out on a date?"

"No, I'm just asking if you want to get a cup of coffee. I want to get one, so I figured I'd ask if you wanted one too. I'm quite happy to go by myself."

"You can't really have a charming conversation by yourself," he said. "I'll join you."

"Why, are you bringing someone with you?" I joked.

"Ooh, sassy. I'll have you know I'm full of charming conversation and intellectual observations."

"Really? You strike me more as the type of guy that headbutts his way through a problem if he get stuck. No offense."

"Hey, a guy can be good at headbutting *and* reading books. I don't have any TV or internet out in my cabin you know? If I want entertainment, I have to read a book, draw, or paint."

"You draw and paint?" I said again, sounding more surprised than I intended to.

"Yeah, the neanderthal can express himself, imagine that," Blake said as we headed out onto the street and in the direction of the nearest coffee place.

"Sorry, I didn't mean it like that. You just surprised me, that's all. I had you down as the type of guy that goes home and spends his night watching football."

"Hey nothing wrong with sports, I'm a big fan."

"Well I guessed one aspect of your personality correctly at least." Blake held the door open for me and we headed inside a coffee shop, ordered two drinks and sat down.

"What about you?" he asked. "What are you doing when you're not solving murders?"

"I also like to read, though I'm not much of an artist. I never actually considered myself much of a creative until I took over the bakery. Before I moved here, I was kind of stuck working dead-end jobs and trying to get out of debt, so I never really had time to pursue any real hobbies."

"Got any lined up now that you're raking in the big bucks?" he joked.

I laughed. "I am *not* raking in the big bucks; we're just about making enough to cover rent and bills. Hopefully with Daphne on board we'll start getting more customers through the door. The mobile bakery van did really well on its first day, I need to get that back on the road, but my attention is always required elsewhere—like today for example."

"You never answered the question," he said firmly, taking a sip of his drink. His dark eyes twinkled, and my heart fluttered for a moment.

"Oh, hobbies? I guess I've got to give knitting a go, right? What self-respecting single lady can't knit? I've always wanted to try ice skating as well, but I've just never had a chance."

Blake's eyes lit up. "Heck, there's a rink in town, what's stopping you? Though as your keeper I'd probably have to stay close by—those blades are a potential threat."

I smirked. "Almost sounds like you're the one asking me on a date now."

Blake held his hands up. "Just making an observation. You never know when those dark witches might strike again, I hear that they love ice skating." Again, I found myself laughing. "What's funny?" Blake asked.

"I dunno, you, I guess. I've not seen this side of you before. You're always so serious and brooding. I prefer you like this, like an actual human."

His smile faltered a little and he looked down at his drink. "Maybe sometimes I get carried away, I'm sorry. I take this job very seriously—protecting you that is—the truth is that keepers in my pack have failed at their missions before and their witches have been killed. Part of me is terrified I'm going to slip up and the same is going to happen to you."

I gulped, not expecting this casual coffee was going to take such a serious turn. "You already saved my butt once, and you did a pretty great job as far as I recall. Don't be so hard on yourself, you're doing a great job. With you and Hudson watching my back I've got nothing to worry about!"

I intended for the comment to lighten the mood a little, but Blake didn't take the bait. "As far as I'm concerned, he's top of the threat list. You might trust him, but I will always keep one eye open around that guy."

"Why? Hudson saved my life too. I don't know why you have to hate each other so much. You're on the same team."

Blake just shook his head. "He's a magically enhanced human, Zora. How much do you know about the organization that pumped him full of that stuff? Because I don't know a damn thing—and that worries me."

"I don't know much either, but they're a secret underground magical organization, it's part and parcel of their territory. They're good guys though."

"Are they?" Blake asked. "I guess I just don't trust people that operate under such intense secrecy. If there's one thing you should know about me, Zora, it's that I have great intuition, and something just feels slightly off about Hudson and the whole MAGE thing."

"He's said the same about you," I pointed out. "I think you both just need to put aside your differences and get along. You'd make a good team, and you might finally get rid of your little flying hedgehog problem."

This time Blake did crack a smile. "I'm still not ready to talk about that."

"I did see a smile though!" I said, pointing at him. Blake's radio crackled to life, Tamara's voice coming over the waves.

"Bobcat this is Crimson Wing, do you copy me, over?"

"I don't remember agreeing to callsigns, over," Blake said.

"I thought it would be fun. Are you with Sparkles, over?"

I jumped in. "Am I Sparkles? I love it, over."

"That you are. I've finished up looking over the scene and I've got some interesting findings. Why don't you both get back here, and I'll go over them with you. Crimson Wing over and out."

Blake looked at the radio unenthusiastically and lifted his gaze to mine. "Why am I bobcat? I hate bobcats! I need a way better callsign."

"I think it's done now, Bobcat, there's no un-ringing that bell."

Blake finished his coffee with one big sip and stood up. "Let's get back to work."

A few minutes later we were back at the crime scene. Tamara had opened up the two large suitcases she had brought along with her, transforming them into a miniature laboratory of sorts.

"Woah, you're not messing around," I said as we stepped into the room. "What is all this stuff?" Tamara's mobile science laboratory looked like something out of a movie.

"This is my old reliable science junk. Obviously all this equipment *does* have proper names, but I find when I start going into detail the normies start falling asleep."

I chuckled. "Fair enough, so what did you find?"

"There are three things that stand out to me," Tamara began.

"Hopefully these clues will give you guys something to go off."

"Let's here them then," Blake said.

"The first one you've probably already noticed, as it's not scientific but more observational. Do you see these bindings on the hands and feet? These are no ordinary knots."

"That's what I said!" Blake perked up at having noticed something. He claimed he wasn't good at detective work, but he obviously had an eye for it.

"You did notice then?" Tamara said. "They're not simple slipknots, whoever tied these things knows their stuff, and they did *not* want these bindings to break—obviously."

"Which one of these fancy machines analyzes knots?" I asked Tamara jokingly.

"That would be this one." She tapped her head. "Self-confessed knot fan here. I even went to knot camp for five consecutive summers!"

"That's… a thing?" Blake asked.

"Oh, for sure. You wouldn't believe some of the stories I have from those wild days, but I'll save them for another time. Don't want to get *tied down* reliving my past!"

Blake and I both groaned at the awful pun. "Uh, so what else did you find?" I asked Tamara.

"I noticed a trace of sticky residue on the handle of the murder weapon." Tamara moved in close to the scene and gestured for us both to do the same. "See this here on the handle?"

"Huh, I didn't notice that," Blake remarked.

"Me neither." I don't know what it was, a light caramel-colored streak that glistened under the light.

"It's cinnamon paste!" Tamara said excitedly. "Whoever killed this guy must have had cinnamon paste on their hands! Could be our killer is a baker."

Blake looked at me in a suggestive way. "You sure you didn't kill this guy?"

"Pretty sure. Keep asking though and I'll gladly add another body into the mix."

Tamara laughed. "The last clue might not be that helpful, but I found dander on the ground and on the victim's clothes. It's cat hair. If he has cats then that explains it, but if he doesn't then it has to come from the killer."

"Did he have cats?" Blake said and looked at me.

"How the heck should I know? I don't know the first thing about him apart from him being an arrogant jerk."

"That's all I've got for now anyway," Tamara said. "I'll take him back to the morgue to do an autopsy, but it probably won't take me long to establish cause of death." Tamara snapped her fingers then and a notepad appeared in her hands. It caught me by surprise because I didn't realize she was a witch.

"You're magical?" I asked with surprise. I hadn't felt a presence of magic around her.

"Barely," she said with a smile while jotting something down in her notepad. "Mom says I was always so interested in science that my magic never had a chance to fully develop. Doesn't bother me particularly, to be honest I do find science way more interesting. Science is predictable and comforting, magic is whacky and chaotic—you never know what's going to happen next!"

Just at that moment a smoking portal opened on the ceiling and Hermes crashed to the floor with a loud shriek. He immediately jumped into a sitting position and started grooming himself, pretending the embarrassing entrance hadn't happened.

"Case in point," Blake mumbled as Tamara started packing away her lab.

"Hermes? What the heck dude? I told Constance I need you over here right away!" I said.

"Yeah, about *that,* I got sidetracked with something else, sorry Zora. I came as soon as I could."

"What could you possibly be up to that was more important than this?" I asked.

"It's a funny story actually, I wanted to see how dark it was inside the clothes hamper, and when I finally managed to get in there, you won't believe this—"

"You fell asleep," I said.

"How did you know?!"

"Call it a hunch. Listen, Kaiser Klaus is dead, and I think he has a magic ring, can you tell me what it is?"

Hermes turned around, his bright eyes widening upon seeing the body. "Ugh, okay, let's have a look then." He moved closer to Kaiser to get a look and peered at the ring on his cold dead hands. A pair of spectacles appeared at the end of Hermes' nose as he examined the thing, and he mumbled to himself.

"Well?" I asked.

"I might be mistaken, but I'm pretty sure it's a Ring of Mordoc." Hermes sat back from the body and his glasses disappeared.

"What does it do?" Blake asked. "And how did a human like Kaiser Klaus happen upon it?"

"Humans stumble upon magic things all the time, they're very talented at finding things they shouldn't. Most of the time it's harmless things, but a ring like this can actually be quite dangerous—he should not have this. It's complicated to explain, but whoever wears this ring can steal positive energy."

"That doesn't sound good," I said.

"No, it's quite unpleasant. You have to expel negative energy for it to work. You could, for example, be mean to someone, make them feel bad about themselves. The ring will then take positive energy from that person, usually in the form of gratitude or worship. That influx of energy will feel like quite the rush—there's a chance this guy didn't know the ring was magical but was addicted to its effects."

"That explains why everyone was acting so weirdly around him then," I said. "All he did was insult people, and they worshipped the ground he walked on." Actually, now that I knew about the ring I felt a lot saner. The way that Zelda and everyone else was acting—there *was* a reason behind it after all.

"Didn't affect you though," Blake noted.

"Yeah, what's that about?" I asked Hermes.

"Well you're a Prismatic Witch, you've got a higher tolerance against this sort of stuff than other people," Hermes explained. It was just as Blake had guessed.

"What about the voodoo woman though? She was the only other person that saw him for what he was."

"Voodoo magic is different, and if it's *real* voodoo magic that is rare in itself. I'd guess your mysterious friend has some sort of protection too."

"What do we do with the ring?" Blake asked. "Seems too dangerous to leave something like this lying around."

"It needs to be destroyed. There are two options." Hermes jumped up onto a chair. "I take it to the highest mountain in Tibet and speak with the great Shang Lok, he can intone an unbinding ceremony and destroy the magic within."

"And what's the second option?" I asked.

"Step on it," Hermes said simply.

"I vote option two," Blake said. He pulled the ring off Kaiser's finger and crushed it under the foot. It made a small explosive sound, and when he pulled his foot back the light in the stone was out.

"One problem solved, ninety million to go," I joked.

"Come on," Blake said to me. "Let's talk to some folk and see if we can dig up any suspects."

"Uh, you're on your own for that one homeboy!" I said. "I've got to get back to the bakery and open for the afternoon. I told you I wasn't going to be on this case twenty-four-seven."

"I can't do this by myself!" Blake complained.

"Take Hermes," I said with a shrug. "He's more than willing to help."

Hermes looked delighted by the idea. "I can magic up a deerstalker!"

"I'll just work it alone," Blake grumbled. "Can't exactly drag a talking cat around with me while I try and solve this thing."

"Zora that means I can come back to the bakery and bother you instead!"

"Oh... great," I said through a hollow smile.

Perhaps I was better off staying here after all?

CHAPTER 11

The next day started normally enough, Daphne and I put the bread fair behind us and got on with business as usual. Even though she'd only been with the bakery for less than a week we already worked really well together, like a well-oiled team that had been a partnership for years.

"Don't get me wrong," Daphne said as we shared a cup of tea downstairs during a quiet moment, "I'm sad that guy is dead, but he couldn't expect to go around talking like that to people without any repercussion!"

"You've changed your tune!" I remarked. Just yesterday Daphne and everyone else in town were lapping up Kaiser Klaus and his horrid little attitude.

"Yes, I don't know what came over me. I knew he was horrible, but I couldn't help trying to please him."

"There was a ring," I said. "A magic ring. It changed how people acted around him. Blake destroyed it yesterday."

"Well that explains it then! That horrible little man had everyone brainwashed? I feel like I need to shower from the way I was acting around him. Is the spell over now the ring is broken?"

"Must be," I observed. "You seem to have snapped out of it at least."

"Any idea who it might have been? Who killed him? I mean that Mistress Bridgette was pretty furious with him." Daphne cleaned her cup in the sink and got ready to go back to work.

"Blake's the one putting a list of suspects together. I think he expects me to run around playing detective with him—I've got to start paying more attention to this place if I want to make a success of things though."

"Hey I used to run Marjorie's old shop by myself all the time. If you've got things to take care of I can hold the fort here," Daphne said.

"Really?" I asked. "You only just started though!"

"True, but I've worked in kitchens before this. They're all sort of the same, though this one is a little more efficient than Marjorie's. I might be getting ahead of myself, but I'm pretty confident I could take care of things solo."

"I'll keep it in mind, thanks. I'm not going to drop you in it today though, today is all about the—"

Just then Zelda burst through the door, breathing heavily. Her hair was all over the place, and she looked like she had sprinted here. "We've got a problem!" she said. "It's Celeste, I think they've taken her!"

"Who?" I asked as Zelda came forward to the counter. It was a good thing the bakery was empty at the moment.

"The sirens! She never showed up for work this morning and I just got this photo, well—look!" Zelda pulled her phone out and showed me a blurry photo on the screen. It was hard to make out, but it looked like the edge of Celeste's head, with several blurry red figures in the background. A message was attached to the photo, though it looked like it had been typed in a hurry, because it didn't make much sense:

SENFFFF HELFFFF!!!!! PIDFINS!!!

"Pidfins?" I asked, looking up at Zelda.

"I think she means sirens; she must have tried to send the message in secret! We have to go and help her, Zora!"

"Where do we find them?"

"There's a hidden cove, they're supposed to have a cave there. We'd have to take a boat. We'll have to get Sabrina too; we can't leave her out of this!"

I looked at Daphne in despair. Only a minute ago I said I wasn't going to abandon her. "Uh so it looks like my cousin might have been abducted by evil mermaids…"

"It's okay, I can look after things here, you go!" Daphne said with encouragement.

"You're a star, thanks Daphne." I turned my attention back on Zelda. "Okay, I'll get the van, you call Sabrina. We'll drive to her shop to pick her up and then try and find a boat."

We ran out of the bakery, two witches on a mission to get their cousin back. I'd suspected these sirens were going to become a bigger problem, I just hadn't anticipated it would happen so soon.

* * *

"I WARNED HER!" Sabrina said as I drove to the lake front. "I warned her not to get involved with the sirens, but did she listen? No!"

"Everything is probably going to be fine," I said, though I honestly had no idea what I was talking about. I was just trying to calm everyone down a little. "How dangerous are these sirens exactly?"

"They're magical creatures in their own right," Sabrina said. "Sirens in general aren't pleasant at the best of times, and the ones we have around here aren't famed for being that friendly."

"I'm trying to gauge what we're walking into here though, can the three of us hold a candle against a group of evil mermaids?"

"I don't know," Sabrina said. "In all honesty I think we're walking into a deathtrap, but we can't just leave Celeste. If they take her into the depths, they'll change her into a siren too!"

"That's not going to happen, so stop worrying about it."

Again, I had no idea if we'd get there in time to stop that from happening, or even if that was why the sirens had taken Celeste in the first place. All I knew is that we had to go in there with a semblance of calm, or this had no chance of going well. We were dealing with dangerous magical creatures here, and I felt like we were at a disadvantage.

An idea came to me then, I passed my phone to Zelda, who was sitting in the passenger seat. "Do me a favor, call Hudson."

"Lover boy? Why?"

"It's basically his job taking care of dangerous magical creatures, this seems like the type of thing that will be right up his alley."

Zelda dialed the number. "Hi, Hudson? No, it's not Zora, it's Zelda, her younger sister. We've met before. I laughed at your jokes and complimented your broad sh—"

"Just put him on speaker!" I scolded her.

Zelda fumbled the phone as I shouted and she put it on speaker. "Zora, is that you?" Hudson asked.

"Yeah, listen we've got a problem. Some mermaids have taken our cousin hostage. Could you help us?"

"It's not the mermaids that live out on the lake, is it?"

"Yes, we have a developing problem with them."

"Okay then listen up, you need to wait for me before you go and visit them. I've been briefed on the local siren population and those guys need to be taken seriously. Do you have a tribute?"

"A what now?"

"A tribute, you need to bring them something if you're going to their cave. If you don't, they'll probably kill you. ...You girls are witches; don't you know this stuff?" he asked.

"Funnily enough mermaid hostage negotiation doesn't come up that often for us," Sabrina shouted from the back.

"Who was that?" Hudson asked.

"My cousin Sabrina. Celeste is her sister. We're in my van now and racing to the lake front to find a boat."

"Okay, I've got a slight change of plan for you. Meet me at the dock by the bottom of Paltino Street, I've got a boat there, we can take that —I'll be there in five minutes."

"That dock's been closed for years!" Zelda shouted. "Ever since the old pier burned down!"

"Just trust me," Hudson said cryptically, and with that he ended the call.

Sabrina and Zelda directed me to the old burned down pier, which was two minutes outside of town heading towards the east. We pulled up in the abandoned lot, and for a moment I wondered if this was another trap set by dark witches.

"Over here," Hudson shouted. We all turned around and saw him standing inside the doorway of an old gaming arcade. We hurried over and followed him inside, heading down a dark corridor.

"McNally's!" Zelda said fondly. "I've not been in here since I was a kid."

"Chances are it might have changed since you were last here," Hudson said, he opened a door and revealed an underground dock filled with all sorts of high-tech looking boats and submersibles. It was like someone had crossed a secret spy hideout with an alien spaceship.

"What is this?!" Sabrina said in amazement.

"This is one of MAGE's tech stashes," Hudson said. "We've got several secret stores so we can respond to emergencies quickly. I've got a boat over here with everything we need, follow me."

We ran over to a sleek black race boat, and all climbed inside, Hudson handed me a black backpack. "This is for you, keep tight hold of it."

"What's inside?" I asked as he moved over to the boat's controls. He pressed a few buttons, moved a large lever forward and the boat accelerated. The wall ahead of us opened and closed again once the boat passed through. Now we were on the open lake Hudson accelerated more and we started moving over the water with great speed.

"Take a look, there's a rainbow conch, a ring of pearls and sea truffle oil. Should be enough to placate our friends for now."

"You just had this stuff to hand?" Sabrina asked with surprise.

"MAGE likes to be prepared, we have supplies prepped and ready to go at a moment's notice for a multitude of magical emergencies. I didn't have mermaid recon on my bingo card for today, but hey, part of the job."

Hudson looked back over his shoulder as he talked to us. There was a big grin on his face, like he was completely in his element handling danger like this. I must admit I was relieved to have him here, I was glad I called him.

"Uh, do we have to sign like a non-disclosure form about all this hidden spy stuff?" Zelda asked.

Hudson just laughed. "Don't worry about it, I'll have to erase the secret base and the boat from your memory after this is done." He paused and looked at me for a moment. I'd been to MAGE HQ once before and Hudson had tried the memory blanking on me then, but it hadn't worked properly. The look he gave me was something along the lines of *I guess I'll just have to trust you.*

Guess so, I thought, looking back at him

Sabrina held her hand up. "Yeah, hi, I do not consent to having my memory blanked."

"Something tells me you won't have a problem when it's done," Hudson pointed out. "Besides, my hands are kind of tied on this one. Its protocol passed down by higher ups at the HQ. If you want my help, then I have to keep our secrets secret."

"We won't tell anyone!" Sabrina said.

"Wait." Zelda sat up straight. "Have you helped us out with things before?"

Hudson grinned. "May well have, I can't really say."

She looked at me. "I remember you saying the memory stuff doesn't work on you. Has he helped us out with magic problems before?"

"No," I said. "Let's move on from the memory blanking, shall we? How long until we get there Hudson?"

"We're about five minutes out. I want you to reach in the back-pack, there's a small blue box with little black pills inside. I need you all to take one and swallow it."

"What do they do?" Sabrina asked as I found the box and opened it. Inside there were a dozen of the little black pills.

"They're called Lanqua tablets, you'll be able to understand the sirens' language. They do speak English, but they have their own language as well, and I want to make sure we understand everything they say. Take the pills and hold on tight, I'm going to speed up on this last stretch."

Zelda, Sabrina and I all looked at one another before taking the pills. It was easy to be wary of Hudson because there was so much mystery surrounding him, but he *was* helping us, and I did trust him. Together we popped the pills in our mouths and swallowed them. Apart from a small vibration in the middle of my head I didn't feel anything else after taking the pill.

Soon after that Hudson slowed the boat down and turned into a small cave hidden amongst the trees on the far east edge of the lake. I would have completely missed it if I'd been in charge of the boat. The boat floated slowly into a dark tunnel mouth, and as we got closer four red humanoid figures rose from the water with long jagged tridents in their hands.

Growing up I'd learned that mermaids were beautiful creatures, attractive women with long hair and a giant fish tail for legs. The creatures in front of us right now weren't anything like that picture, and the most human thing about them was their silhouette.

They were rust red, their eyes narrow slits containing dark and alien pupils. Their teeth reminded me of a piranha, and there were no ears at all, just spiky frills on either side of their head. Barnacles clung to their skin and some of them had shells and seaweed around them as some sort of fashion.

And then there was their tales, long and shimmering, thick and covered in bright scales that looked sharp to the touch. I couldn't see the bottom of the tails as they were in the water, but the four sirens had come up out of the water by quite a long way, elevated on their tails like columns so that we were looking up at them. I estimated the tails were probably 20 feet long from their waists.

"Stop right there," a siren in the middle said. His sharp black eyes were focused right on Hudson. "What are you doing here human?"

"We come bringing tribute," Hudson said calmly. My heart was beating in my chest, and I could tell that Zelda and Sabrina were scared out of their wits too. Hudson however looked like he was talking with a gas station attendant. "We believe you have one of our friends."

The four sirens immediately drew back and convened with one another in low hushed voices. A series of clicks made up most of the talk, combined with a strange chittering sound from the spiky frills on their heads.

I felt a faint vibration in my head and the alien sounds started to become English.

"...and somehow, they know!"

"They must have a spy. We should kill them now."

"Bring them to Edra, we can take more to the depths."

Hudson looked back at the three of us with a knowing glance. He could tell we were out of our element here. "Everybody take it easy," he whispered to us. "We'll be fine."

"Enough whispering!" one of the sirens snapped as the group broke out of their huddle. "We will review the tribute first. If it is satisfactory you may speak with our queen. If it is not, we will kill you and eat you."

"Seems fair," Hudson said calmly. "Zora?" I passed Hudson the bag and he held it out over the bow of the boat. One of the sirens swam forward and hooked the bag on the end of its trident. It quickly returned to its group, and they inspected the contents of the bag. Though they didn't say anything at first, the way they looked at the rainbow conch told me they were impressed.

"Your tribute is suitable!" one of them hissed. "You will not die right at this moment. Follow us inside, you shall speak with the queen."

"Man, this place is getting one star when I review it online," Sabrina muttered under her breath.

"Sabrina don't be rude!" Zelda hushed back. "You always have to give at least two stars."

"Why don't we see if we make it out of here alive first?" I said to them both.

"Good idea." Hudson pushed the lever on the boat and we moved forward into the darkness of the sirens' lair.

CHAPTER 12

The path to the lair was long and winding, an expansive network of natural underground canals that were beautiful in a strange and terrifying way. As we journeyed deeper into the darkness, I noticed that the cave walls on either side of us stretched up higher and higher until the craggy rock ceiling overhead disappeared into shadow.

I noticed the water was rushing with a steady current now, moving down on a slight decline. "Where are we?" I whispered to Hudson.

"This cave network goes deep underground; I think we're somewhere underneath the town by this point."

Bright lights on Hudson's boat cut through the darkness, but Sabrina, Zelda and I had each pulled our wands out and summoned a small light incantation to further illuminate the shadow. More sirens appeared as we journeyed through the caves, four of them swimming ahead of the boat as a guide, and four more at the rear to flank us.

"They seriously creep me out," Sabrina said under breath.

I think we all felt that way.

After fifteen minutes the stretch of water we were on finally came to an end at a rocky cove. We were in a massive underground chamber, the air oppressively cold and damp. The sirens slithered onto the ground, their tails moving underneath them like large snakes. "Out of the boat," the commanding siren ordered. "Edra is this way."

The four of us got out of the boat and walked in a closely knit group, surrounded by sirens. They led us to what looked like a blank section of cave wall and stopped. One of them slithered up to the wall, knocked the bottom of their trident against the ground and began speaking in a language I couldn't understand at all.

"Eradok," Hudson whispered to me. "Even the pills can't help with that, it's ancient merfolk magic."

"Silence!" one of the guards hissed. I looked forward at the siren chanting in the unknown tongue, its trident began glowing and then a huge stone archway appeared on the wall. An ornate sculpted frame surrounded the entrance, with various stone sirens carved upon the face. "Through here!"

The archway led us into another magnificent chamber, filled to the brim with mountains of sparkling pearls and the most amazing-colored shells. A clear pathway had been left down the middle of the chamber, and at the far end I saw a group of sirens relaxing in a pool of brilliant azure water.

The guards ushered us forward to the pool, at the center of which there was a sparkling white plinth with a throne upon its top. Sitting on that throne was another siren, but they were adorned with shimmering gemstones and rubies.

"Kneel," Hudson whispered. We all dropped to one knee and a silence came over the chamber.

"Intruders, Queen Edra," one of our accompanying sirens announced. "Though they come bringing tribute."

Edra rose from her sparkling white throne, her dark eyes surveying us with interest. She regarded the tribute and nodded. The guard took the gifts away, no doubt to add them to the mountains of treasure in the room.

"Speak then," the bejeweled siren said. Her body glittered with the dressing of jewels and stones. One piece in particular stood out, though I didn't know why—a necklace around her throat made of silver links and black crystals. "Why does a human and three witches think it fit to cross into the domain of the merfolk?"

"We have reason to believe you have one of our friends captive," Hudson said. "A friend of mine, family to the witches here with me now."

Edra stared at Hudson for a long moment. The sirens looked so unusual to me I couldn't even begin to guess what she was thinking. "We have your friend, and we have her mate too. I would like to know how you traced them here."

"Magic," I said. In reality we only knew Celeste was in danger because she'd managed to message us a photo, but if the sirens found that out, I didn't want to risk getting her into trouble.

Edra seemed displeased with the answer. "Witches, they cannot be trusted! I would not have brought one back here if it wasn't necessary! Be quick and tell me what you want—you would not have come here if you didn't seek something."

"Give back my sister," Sabrina said. "And her 'mate' too. We know you want Gordo, but he has a land-wife, and by your rules you cannot take a human if they are wed."

"By our rules we cannot take a human away from their betrothed," Edra said. "We were most disappointed when our friend wed that witch girl. We planned to convert him to one of our own—and we still do!"

"But the rules are clear," Hudson said. "You can't take him if he's wed, so we ask you return them both."

Edra shook her head. "No, our rules dictate we cannot take a human from their betrothed, and we haven't. We took both of them together."

Hudson opened his mouth and then closed it again. I knew what he was thinking. *Damn, so they're playing the loophole card now?*

"Why do you want them?" I asked.

The siren queen turned her black eyes on me. "Excuse me?"

I repeated the question. "Why do you want them? They're human, and they don't want to leave their world, so why take them?"

"You dare question my intentions?" the queen said, rising up on her red tail. The spiky frills on the sides of her head chittered slightly.

"No," I said firmly, "I just want to understand what your motivations are." I swallowed down the nerves in my throat, refusing to look away from the strange aquatic creature. I didn't want to betray my worry, something told me it was important to stand my ground with this woman.

"The fault lies entirely with you—and by that, I mean the lure of the land. Our numbers are beginning to dwindle. Just this last month two of our own have left the tribe for the very first time, they have gone onto land to live as humans. We have pleaded with them to come back, but they are steadfast in their foolishness. So, we must take two from you, to recuperate our numbers."

"That's no fault of Gordo or Celeste," Zelda pointed out. "You can't take people against their will. Your members left of their own accord!"

Once again Edra's eyes flashed with murderous disapproval, the frills chittering in a way that made my blood run cold. "Watch your tongue witch, if you wish to leave here with your lives, I recommend you be very careful."

"Let's take it easy," Hudson said carefully, holding his hands out to steady the waters. "We don't want a fight here; we just want our friends back."

"Not possible—" Edra dismissed. "We need to regrow our numbers."

An idea came to me then. "What if I find the two that left your tribe? I'll speak to them, convince them to come back."

Edra let out a strange and inhumane laugh. "A weakling witch cannot steer the strong mind of a siren."

"But if we *could* convince them," Hudson cut in quickly. "Get them to return, would you free our friends?"

The siren queen said nothing for a long moment, then she and a small number of her inner circle slithered away to discuss the proposition in their language quietly. Even with the pills my ears couldn't pick up their whispering. After several minutes of discussion, the group disbanded, and Edra looked upon us once more.

"Return the two missing from our number *and* bring more tribute, then we have a deal."

"They come with us now," Sabrina said. "Humans cannot survive down here, it's too cold."

"Rest assured they are kept well. We know that humans are weak and need warmth to live. They have comfortable living arrangements and plenty of food until we take them to the depths."

"Let us take one," Hudson bargained. "The witch. A display of your wisdom and generosity."

Edra blinked as she considered the proposition. "Very well, but if you do not keep up your end of the deal, we will kill the remaining human."

"That's... fair enough." Although Hudson was playing it cool, I got the impression he had no intention of letting Gordo die.

With a motion of her head one of the guards disappeared in a side room and came back a moment later with Gordo and Celeste. From the look on Celeste's face, I could tell she was glad to see us. Despite being captives of the sirens, it seemed they had been looked after.

Edra addressed them. "Your tricky witch friends have come to make a bargain. In return for the members the land has stolen from us, you and your friend shall be freed. One of you may temporarily leave—the witch, Gordo, you shall remain."

"We can't leave him here!" Celeste said. "Not on his own!"

"That is the deal," Edra said coldly. "Take it or leave it."

"Eh, it's fine." Gordo patted Celeste on the shoulder and smiled. "I've spent plenty of time down in these caves before they took me as prisoner. The food is always good, and they look after humans—even if they come across as short."

Gordo may have been fine with the idea, but I could tell Celeste didn't like it. Still, with little other choice she walked over to us. Sabrina swamped her in a huge hug.

"You have five tides to complete our arrangement," Edra said. "Leave now, and do not go back on our deal. We will come and take you all if necessary."

We began walking back through the chamber of aquatic treasure, the air thick with tension. On the way back to the lake I expected the sirens to go against their word and attack us. I had my wand out and I noticed everyone else did too, but sure enough the strange creatures stayed true to their word and let us leave.

When we finally pulled back out onto the open lake the sunlight was blinding, I took a huge gulp of air and felt myself relax for the first time in an hour. "I can come back for Gordo at sundown if you like," Hudson proposed. "I can sneak in and out of those caves without them noticing me."

"He can do that?!" Celeste said eagerly.

"I suspect you *can* do that," I said to Hudson, "but I don't think we should play things that way at all. It won't make our problem any better, will it?"

He shook his head. "No, it won't, most likely it will only make them worse. The fact that sirens are taking humans from land in the first place is very bad though. It's unusual, even for a pack as hostile as this one. Sirens hardly ever interfere with human populations, so I think something else is going on here."

Soon after that we got back to Hudson's secret underground dock. He escorted us back to the van in the parking lot and when I blinked, we were somewhere completely different altogether, a coffee shop near Compass Cove's central park, only around the corner from my bakery.

"Wait a second," Sabrina said vaguely, "how did we get here?"

I looked at Hudson and realized what had happened. "You blanked our memories?"

"Yes, sorry. I told you I can't leave any trace of MAGE's secret locations, but you should remember everything else about the arrangement."

"I think I feel a little sick," Zelda said. She did look a concerning shade of green.

"That'll pass, have some of the gingerbread," Hudson advised. Looking down I saw a plate chock full of cakes. We all reached forward and grabbed something.

"How are we supposed to track down two missing sirens and return them?" Zelda asked through a mouthful of chocolate cupcake.

"That… I don't quite know yet," Hudson said. "Merfolk have the ability to transition into humans so they can walk on land, but as of this moment we have no way of tracing them. They also don't do it very often."

"Well, we have to think of something!" Celeste said. "We can't just leave Gordo down there!"

"Don't worry." I put my hand on Celeste's shoulder. "We're going to fix all of this. Someone in this town must know how to find merfolk in human form."

"I might know someone," Sabrina said as she bit a chunk out of a cookie. We all looked at her.

"Really?" Hudson asked with intrigue.

"Yeah, well—I know the type of person. We need a sea witch. I bet they'd be able to help us with something like this."

"Great, now we just have to find a sea witch," Zelda muttered.

"Is that hard?" I asked. Hudson had the same querying look on his face.

"They're reclusive, and not all that common. How many can there be in Compass Cove?" Celeste asked. "Three, maybe four?"

"Six," Sabrina answered through another mouthful of cookie.

"You know?!" Zelda asked in surprise.

"Of course I know, I run the only wand shop in town. I've practically met every witch that lives around here. If I haven't sold them a wand, I've serviced them."

"Can you connect us with one?" I asked her. "It might be our only way of tracking these merfolk."

"Possibly," she said. "If you think the sirens are unfriendly then wait until you meet a sea witch—they are the kings of the introverts. Of the six I know I think four of them are an immediate no, and as for the last two—" Sabrina paused as she considered something. "Actually, I think there's only one that would possibly agree to helping us, but even that is a tall order."

"When can you let us know?" I asked.

"Give me a day and I'll reach out to her, see if I can set something up. I'm not making any promises."

"Well, if this is all settled for now, I think I'll be going." Hudson stood up and brushed himself off. "There's still a Tizzie-Whizzie on the loose, and I'm overdue for getting my ass kicked. Zora, get in touch when we have a plan."

"Will do," I said. "Thanks again for the help." Hudson left and I noticed Sabrina, Celeste and Zelda were all staring at me in a strange way. "What?" I asked.

"You love him!" Sabrina said in a sing-song voice.

"Thank you, Hudson, I'll call you when I want babies!" Zelda mocked.

"Kiss me Hudson, kiss me in your secret base!" Celeste joined in.

"I should have left you all in that cave," I grumbled.

CHAPTER 13

"You should have called me, I could have helped you with those darn sirens, everyone around here respects ol' Hermes!"

"Is that so?" I said and took a bite of my breakfast pastry. "Something tells me you would have taken one look at them and ran in the opposite direction—they weren't exactly friendly."

"Bah, like I'm afraid of a few fish folk. You know people used to call me The Amazing Hermes? I was the wizard of a generation!"

"And now you're in a cat's body, sitting on an avocado pillow next to a radiator. Time's change."

"I'm still fierce!" Hermes protested. "I'd do a lot more around here if I just got a little respect!"

I smirked again. "I believe you Hermes. A lot of people take you for granted around here." Sometimes the easiest way to get him to stop talking was to tell him what he wanted to hear.

"Finally! A little bit of recognition!"

"Any idea how I can track down these missing sirens then?" I asked him.

"Huh?" Hermes looked at me with one of his legs stuck in the air, he had just started cleaning himself.

"The sirens, how would you deal with the problem?"

Hermes thought about the question for a long moment. "I mean, I don't have ideas right at this moment, you kind of caught me on the back foot here!"

I laughed. "Of course, of course. Well you come to me when something comes to mind."

Not long after that Daphne arrived for the morning preparation, and we started getting the bakery ready for the day. A few hours later we flipped the door sign to 'open' and the busy morning began. Bringing Daphne on and introducing her new bakes had really been a breath of fresh air to the shop, our customer numbers had jumped significantly since she'd come on board.

Halfway to noon I went upstairs for a quick tea break in the apartment. I'd just sat down with my cup of tea when Daphne shouted up to me from downstairs.

"Hey, there's a cop here to see you. Says it's about work?"

I put my cup down on the table and sighed. Blake. "Send him up!" I shouted to her.

Blake came up the stairs and stepped into the apartment. "Morning."

"Morning. Not wearing any shades today?"

"The eyes finally healed over," he said.

"I half expected some new injuries from your little winged-hedgehog problem."

"Uh yeah, I'm not going near that thing again." Blake chuckled nervously and took a seat at the table with me. "I'll leave it to your little magical friend."

"Want a drink?" I asked him.

"Coffee would be great, thanks."

I got up and poured him a cup from the pot and then sat at the table again. "Go on then, spit it out, I know this isn't a social call."

Blake sipped his drink and put it down. "I've made a little headway with the case; I've even got a few suspects. I was hoping you might come out with me today and help me speak to them."

"Why me?" I asked.

"Because you're good at that type of thing, and I struggle to keep a lid on my emotions sometimes."

"Wow, we're finally saying it out loud?" I said and smirked. "Are you on a nine-step program or something?"

Blake looked at me and rolled his eyes. "I know you think I'm a hot head, but you should see some of the other members of my pack. I was awarded the privilege of being a keeper because I'm generally regarded as being level-headed amongst my wolf kin."

I lifted my brows in surprise. "I'm intensely curious to see what the rest of them are like then."

"You can meet them sometime, if you want to of course."

"...Sure, that would be nice."

Blake took another quick sip of his drink. "Look I'm trying to be better, it's not always easy keeping you're cool when you're like me."

"What do you mean by that?"

"Being a werewolf," he said in a low voice. "I literally have a wolf inside me, Zora. There's a lot of anger, rage, and energy. I try and let it all out in wolf form, but it can be hard. I'm not suited to towns like this, I need open-air and space to get my paws on the ground."

"I think I understand," I said. "Sorry for being judgmental, I can imagine it's hard being away from your natural territory."

"I'm fine, honestly, but I wish you could see the real me—I'm a lot more mellow out in the sticks. Anyway, I wanted your help because I'm not so good at getting answers out of people without resorting to extreme measures."

"I had noticed," I said with another smile. "Who's the suspect then?"

"There's three actually, and one of them is the woman you identified the other day. Mistress Bridgette? She's due a visit. So, what do you say? Care to help a friend out?"

I tapped my fingers on the desk as I considered the idea. "I'll have to run it past Daphne first, she's still new here and I already left her on her own yesterday."

Of course, Daphne didn't have a problem with handling things by herself, so I left the bakery with Blake and climbed into his cruiser. I made a mental note to myself that Daphne would definitely be getting a raise at the end of the month. Now she was around I was able to keep the bakery open *and* deal with all the random problems my day-to-day life threw at me.

"Sorry again for pulling you away," Blake said. "I don't want to mess this up though, and you seem like my best bet. How's the new hire going?"

"She's great actually, she's definitely making my life easier. Once I've got a bit more money coming in, I want to hire a few more people, I need someone that can take the van out each day and sell things on the road. We made good money doing that before the local paper made everyone afraid of me by calling me a murderer."

Thankfully that was water under the bridge now and my name had been cleared. People were slowly starting to come back to the bakery, but that wound still hadn't finished healing.

"Got your eye on anyone?" Blake asked.

"I've done a couple of interviews now and most of them were train wrecks. There was one other applicant that looked great on paper, but she never turned up to the interview."

"Well, that's a red flag in itself," Blake said. "By the way, there was something else I wanted to talk to you about. Your antics yesterday, did you think that wouldn't get back to me?"

"Are you talking about the sirens?" I asked. He nodded. "I'd ask how you even know, but it figures seeing as how I don't get any privacy around here."

"I would have been there to help you if I wasn't tied down with policework. I didn't think this disguise would turn into an actual job —I might have to can it. Do you know how dangerous sirens are? What were you thinking going out there?"

"I had Sabrina and Zelda with me, and Hudson was there too. He was a great help actually; I don't think we would have been so fortunate without him."

Glancing over I saw Blake's jaw tense as I mentioned Hudson. "Still, I'd rather you didn't go putting yourself in dangerous situations like that. You could have been hurt."

"So could my cousin Celeste, that's why we went to rescue her."

"Fair point," Blake grumbled. "So, what's happening with the sirens then?"

I filled Blake in on the deal we had made with the strange lake creatures. He listened carefully as I explained it all from start to finish. "So now we have to find a sea witch and *then* we can find these missing sirens that moved onto land... it's a big mess."

Blake's hand moved over the wheel as we turned onto another street. "I'm going to keep a very close eye on this moving forward. I don't trust sirens, and I don't like that Hudson is the one spearheading the operation."

"Enough talk about Hudson and all the things you don't like about him. Where are we driving to? Who's our first suspect?"

"We are heading to Compass Cove Climbing Center, our first suspect is a Mr. Gareth Taylor," Blake explained.

"Who is he, and why is he a suspect?"

"After you left the convention center the other day, I talked to everyone in Kaiser Klaus' entourage, asked them who might have had reason to hurt him. One name kept coming up, Gareth Taylor. He's Kaiser's former assistant—apparently in the early days he did a lot of the groundwork and helped to get Kaiser's brand up and running."

"Why is he a suspect though?"

"Kaiser fired him just over a month ago—apparently there wasn't really a solid reason. He told everyone else that Taylor wasn't pulling his weight and was 'overdue' a sacking, but everyone I spoke to said he was a great employee—no one had a bad word to say about the guy."

"Why would Kaiser Klaus fire him then?" I pondered out loud.

"My thoughts exactly but get this—Gareth Taylor was due a huge contractual bonus for meeting targets set by Kaiser. Just before Kaiser was due to pay them, he fired him instead."

"Yup, that would do it. Was this assistant at the bread fair though? He didn't have reason to be there if he'd been fired."

"I don't know, we'll have to go and ask him when we get there. It was a public convention though, nothing to stop the guy from showing up."

"Do we have any surveillance footage from the backstage area?" I asked.

"No cameras around there," Blake said with a shake of his head. "I already checked. No one else in Kaiser's entourage recalls seeing Gareth Taylor at the convention either, but it's possible he blended in with the crowd."

A few minutes later we pulled into the parking lot shadowed by a large warehouse. The climbing center was deceptively larger on the inside, a playground of tall colored walls covered in a rainbow assortment of handholds.

"This place looks fun!" I said as we walked over to the reception. It wasn't super busy at the moment, but there were half a dozen people climbing different courses throughout the building. There were large crashmats on the floor to catch anyone that fell.

"Welcome to—" a cheery young girl began behind the desk. She was halfway through eating a huge pastry covered in white frosting. The girl set it down on a napkin and had a drink to clear her mouth. "Sorry about that, can't function without my morning Cinnabon, let me try again. Welcome to Compass Cove Climbing Center! Are you climbing or bouldering today?"

"Bouldering?" I asked.

"We've got the shorter walls on the left side of the warehouse just there," she said, pointing behind her. "You can climb them without ropes and there are crashmats to catch you when you jump off. It's a pretty good way to start out if you're learners." The girl looked at Blake and paused. "You seem quite built though, have you got much climbing experience?"

"I uh… no, I work out in a gym. Moving weights up and down. Lifting iron, you know, that sort of thing?" I gave Blake a perplexed look. He reminded me of an alien trying to explain how a gym worked. Something told me his size and strength came entirely from his powers, and from his explanation alone it didn't sound like he'd ever set foot in a gym.

"...Right. Anyway, my name is Maddie, I'm the manager here at the center. What can I get you guys started with?"

"We're actually here to speak with a Mister Gareth Taylor," Blake said. "Is he around?"

"Gareth?" Maddie said, she looked slightly taken aback. "Is something wrong?"

"We're working a murder case. Gareth's old employer was killed the other day—we're speaking to people close to him to try and find out more information."

"That's awful! I don't know if Gareth would be able to help you much, he's not spoken with his old boss since he was fired. Real jerk move if you ask me." Maddie picked up her pastry and took another bite.

"You know about that?" I asked her.

"Of course, Gareth and I are seeing each other—we've been together for a while now. As soon as I heard that jerk fired him, I offered him a job here. This is where we first met actually."

"Congratulations," Blake said, sounding like he couldn't care any less. "So where is Gareth?"

"He's on the floor, just doing a training session with a client. I'll get someone else to cover him if you need to talk."

"That would be great, thanks. Is there any where we can talk in private?"

"You can use my office, just up the steps on your right!"

A few minutes later we sat down at the table in Maddie's office with Gareth. He was a lanky young man with a receding hairline and a large hook nose.

"I figured you might want to talk to me," he said as he joined us at the table.

"Why's that?" Blake asked.

"Well, I knew Kaiser better than anyone. I was his assistant for five years! Morning to night I was there for that guy, even if he didn't show much thanks for it. What did you want to know?"

"I spoke with a few people at the convention center," Blake began,

"I asked them who might have reason to hurt Kaiser Klaus—quite a few people mentioned your name."

Gareth scoffed. "Because the guy fired me? That was over a month ago! If I wanted revenge, I would have done it a lot sooner!"

"You don't seem very surprised to hear about his passing," I mentioned.

Gareth turned his attention on me. "I heard about it the day it happened, I'm still in a group chat with some of my old work pals—Kaiser might have been a pain in the butt, but I had some good friends there. I was in shock when I heard, just ask Maddie, she'll vouch for me!"

"From what we hear Kaiser fired you right before you were due a huge bonus," Blake recapped. "Everyone said you helped build Kaiser's brand from the ground up, and right before you're due your reward he kicks you to the curb. That must have made you pretty angry."

"It *did* make me angry, but like I'm not a freaking lunatic. I didn't murder the guy. Besides, I was nowhere near the convention center on the day of the bread fair, I was working here all day, you can check the camera footage! Maddie will be able to show you!"

"Could she do that now?" Blake asked.

"Absolutely!"

Gareth shouted down to his girlfriend and Blake went with her to check the surveillance footage, leaving me alone with Gareth. It was a deliberate move for Blake to leave and me to stay, I wanted Gareth to feel like the interrogation was on momentary pause.

"Sorry to get all up in your grill about this," I said. "I can tell you're a good guy, we just have to rule out all options of course, you understand?"

"Of course," Gareth said, relaxing a little into the moment. "Are you a detective or something? You don't have a uniform like the other guy."

"Uh, in an unofficial capacity. I've helped the police out with a few cases recently. So how are you liking the new job?"

"It's a lot less stressful than my old one. Took a bit of a pay cut as well, but I've always loved climbing—I jumped at the chance when

Maddie made me the offer. Plus, I get to spend a lot more time with her now too."

"You been together long?" I asked.

"Going on a few years now. I was going to use the money from that bonus to get a nice ring and have her make me an honest man, but I'll have to save up a little longer."

"Kids?" I leaned back in my chair.

"Not yet, just a cat and a Roomba," he chuckled. "Pair of them never stop fighting!"

Looking around the office I saw a little display cabinet with some trophies upon it. There were framed photographs with Maddie and other employees from the climbing center. "You girlfriend is quite the climber it seems?" I said.

"Oh, those? They're not for climbing." Gareth chuckled and brought one of the trophies over. The engraving on it said 'Maddie Frank, Slingies Champion 2021'.

"Slingies?" I asked.

"It's a little game that climbers play. You make a tin can pyramid, get yourself a climbing clip and put it on the end of some rope. Stand back ten feet, spin your clip around and sling it into the stack of tins as hard as you can! It's a whole lot of fun, we like to play it when the center is quiet. The competition started as a joke, but it's become a tradition over the years. Maddie always cleans up! She would have been a force to be reckoned with in the wild west!"

"I bet." I laughed and then let out a fake yawn. "Say, do you know where I can get a good danish around here? I missed breakfast this morning and I need a sugar kick."

"There's a little cart on the corner of the block, everyone here rates it highly."

"Got anything you'd recommend?" I asked.

"Oh, I'm not a sweet snacks kind of guy," Gareth said. He held up his left forefinger and pinched it. "I'm diabetic. One too many sweet pastries and I'm on a slippery slope to a coma. Maddie could give you a recommendation or two, she loves that place!"

Not long after that Blake and Maddie returned. "Footage is all good," Blake said as he stepped into the room. "Mister Taylor was here all day. I think we can cross his name off our list."

"That settles it then, thank you both for your time." I stood up from the table and made my way back to the cruiser with Blake. "Who's next?" I asked him.

"Want to check out this strange voodoo woman? She's the most likely culprit in my eyes."

"I have the same feeling too," I said. "She's already on my 'unusual people' list."

Blake smirked and started the car. "A town like this? There's got to be a lot of people on a list like that."

"Yeah, and your name is right at the top!"

He laughed and shook his head. "Well, I walked right into that one."

CHAPTER 14

"What do we really think about Gareth Taylor then?" Blake asked as he pulled into a space just down the street from the voodoo bakery.

"Didn't you just tell him he was off the list?"

"Well yeah, but that was just clever police deception," he said with a knowing wink. "I want to hear what you think."

"I already know what I think, I'd like to hear what junior detective has on his mind."

"Seriously?" Blake asked. "I brought you along for help!"

"I know that, but you're never going to get a hang of this detective business if I spoon feed you all the answers. What did we learn while we were in there?"

Blake turned off the car and drummed his fingers on the wheel. "I'd say the surveillance footage alone is sign enough that the guy is innocent. The cameras showed him in the climbing center all day."

"Yup," I said with a nod. "That's certainly provides him with an alibi for a good chunk of the day but what else did we learn?"

"He had pretty good motive to want him dead... but he didn't have the means of killing the guy."

"Let's ignore the camera footage for a moment and pretend we can't prove he was at the climbing center. What makes you think he might have done it?"

Blake scratched his head and let out a sigh. "Oh, he's good with knots!"

"There we go," I said. "Not only did he say he's been a climbing fan for years, but he'd have to know how to tie several different knots to be a certified climbing trainer. Anything else you picked up on?"

Again he thought then shook his head. "No, that's about it."

"When you were out of the room, I asked him a couple of personal questions. He has a cat, and there was cat dander at the crime scene. There's another big mark against him though."

"What's that?" Blake asked.

"He's diabetic, not likely to touch sweet treats. Tamara said there was cinnamon paste on the handle. There's no reason a diabetic like Gareth would go near something like that. Of course, we *are* ignoring the key piece of evidence in all this—he was at work, so it couldn't have been him."

"You squeezed a lot of information out of that guy, I didn't even realize," Blake said. "I *have* to get better at this."

"Well, here's your chance. Let's speak to Mistress Bridgette and see what she has to say for herself."

We climbed out of the cruiser and made our way down the alleyway to Mistress Bridgette's voodoo bakery. A huge line of people were queued up outside the shop, and from the looks of things the line went all around the block.

"Wow, it looks pretty popular," Blake noted.

"It's been like this every day since she opened. Sabrina and I think she might be brainwashing people somehow."

"Can voodoo do that?" Blake asked as we reached the front of the line.

"I don't actually know, but something is afoot!"

"Excuse me, police business," Blake said to a man waiting in the doorway, he was blocking our entry.

"Wait your turn like everyone else buddy!" the guy said, he then looked at Blake and noticed his size. He shrank back considerably.

"Step aside or I put your head through the window," he said with a low snarl. The man let out an unusual squeak and moved aside to let us through.

"Thanks!" I said cheerily.

The inside of the bakery was packed with customers. Mistress Bridgette was behind the counter with two other staff members, who were moving quickly to get through the line. She saw us enter the shop.

"Ah, I thought I might see you again Miss Wick," she said. "Finally come to try out the wares?"

"Actually, we're here to speak to you about Kaiser Klaus," Blake said. "Do you have a minute?"

"Anything for an officer of the law," Mistress Bridgette said warmly. "Come around the counter and follow me. The office is upstairs."

We followed Bridgette upstairs and found a surprisingly boring office. I'd half expected the unusual voodoo theme to continue into the bones of the bakery, but the small room was unremarkably dull.

"Do you like red leaf tea? We just received a beautiful shipment," she said as she took a seat across the table from us.

"Not for me, thanks," Blake said and also took a seat.

"Me neither," I said and joined them. I looked around at the beige office. "This... isn't what I expected," I remarked.

Bridgette laughed. "What were you picturing? Heads in jars and rope nets hanging from the ceiling? I told you the décor downstairs is just for show, people eat that stuff up."

"Judging from the lines around the block you're not wrong," Blake observed. "I hear business has been good."

"It's been booming. Goes to show what a little bit of market research can do. This town was missing a niche bread shop, and I knew my little offering would fit in just perfectly. Zora, you haven't tried any of my wares yet, care to sample something?"

"I'm good thanks, I usually stuff my face when I'm setting up the shop in the morning." I also had a suspicion I might fall under a spell if I tried some of the food here—everyone else in town felt possessed to wait in line for some reason—the food couldn't be that good, right?

"Suit yourself, so what did you want to talk about then?"

"Kaiser Klaus," Blake said as he took point. "We're working a murder case and trying to figure out how he ended up dead."

"Oh, and what would I know about that?"

"I have it on good authority that you weren't in the best of moods with Klaus on the day he died. Apparently, you threatened to kill him?"

Bridgette looked at me with a smile on her face. She definitely felt different today, acting more like a familiar friend than a morally ambiguous witch. "Is this your doing, Zora? All because of what I said to you?"

"You *did* say you were going to kill him," I pointed out.

Bridgette threw her head back and laughed. "I said the same about my dogs the other day when they tore up my brand-new kitchen cabinets!"

"Dogs?" Blake asked.

"Two big Dobermans. Used to have a parrot too, but he passed." She crossed her chest. "Love you Pandy!"

"Got an owl myself," I said. "And a cat."

Bridgette shivered. "Owls are fine, can't stand cats though. Never liked the things."

"So, Klaus," Blake said, bringing the conversation back on topic. "You were angry with him?"

"Look, that little shrewd man got under my skin. I'll admit I let my tongue run free, but mercy be, I'm not the kinda' woman to run someone down!" She looked at me. "You were just as angry with him as I recall—actually as I remember we were the only ones not sucking up to the man! I suspect there was some weird magic going on."

Blake and I looked at one another. "There was a magic ring," I revealed. "Klaus gained energy from being horrible to people, and in return it made people adore him."

"Ah, that explains it then. No nonsense magic ring like that is gonna cut through my voodoo. I shield myself from flimsy little curses like that. What about you? How come it didn't effect you?"

"I uh... I have magical immunities," I said. I still didn't see Mistress Bridgette as someone I could trust, so I didn't want to tell her about my Prismatic abilities.

"That so?" she said slowly, looking at me through disbelieving eyes. "Well, keep your secrets to yourself. Whatever you're doing, it's wise to keep it up, humans shouldn't have rings like that, and it doesn't surprise me he wound up dead. Way he was talking to people, it was going to happen sooner or later."

"You know what, I think she has a point," Blake said, leaning forward to put his elbows on the table. "I don't think Mistress Bridgette here is our suspect."

"No?" I asked. As of this moment we hadn't learned enough to rule her out, but I understood what Blake was doing. "I think you're right. Sorry for bringing this to you, Bridgette."

Bridgette waved her hand through the air as though it didn't matter. "No need to apologize. Bakers bake, policemen ask questions —it's all a part of the greater cycle."

"Now that I think about it you left the fair early, so you couldn't have been the one to kill him," I said.

"That's right, walked out after he insulted my cooking for the second time. I figured there was better ways of wasting my day."

"Say, I've been curious about these things," Blake said and pointed at a small voodoo fetish doll sitting on top of a pen cup on Bridgette's desk. The little doll was the only voodoo item in the whole room, it was made of knotted black twine and had little white eyes. "How do they work?"

"The fetish? It's very simple. The doll represents someone—it's a conduit for voodoo magic."

"And you can use these things to hurt people?" Blake asked. Bridgette looked at him like he'd grown a second head.

"No, the type of voodoo I practice is protective. Real voodoo is a white magic—ignore all that nonsense you see on the TV. It's not accurate."

"Oh, I see, sorry for getting it wrong," Blake said. "Could you show me how to make one?"

She laughed. "No, I'm afraid not. Frances on the desk could show you when we're not busy, I'm afraid my hands aren't up to the intricate little work no more." Bridgette then held up her hands, and for the first time I realized her fingers were curled up tight with arthritis. "Even the voodoo couldn't stop them from seizing up. Still, I can manage most of the baking, but I need a lot more help these days."

"What's your best seller?" Blake asked. "What keeps people coming back? I love anything with cinnamon in it."

"No cinnamon here," she said. "We're a savory bakery, officer. Our most popular item at the moment is our chili and onion bread. I'll get you two to go! Did you have any other questions?"

Blake looked at me, but I shook my head. I think he'd covered it all quite well. I had to admit that Mistress Bridgette had passed the test with flying colors, but for some reason I still couldn't bring myself to trust her—she *was* hiding something from me, I just knew it.

* * *

A FEW MINUTES later Blake and I were back in his cruiser. He opened the paper bag, pulled out our complimentary chili roll sandwiches and handed one to me. "Come on, let's see what all the fuss is about."

"And become another one of her zombie customers? I don't think so. I'm not lining up around the block every morning like some idiot! I've got things to do."

Blake shrugged his shoulders and took a massive bite of the sandwich. For a few seconds he said nothing, then he looked at me. "You have to try it, it's great."

I stared at the sandwich in my hand, wondering if I should eat it or not. I felt no magical presence coming from the food, it *did* however smell amazing. "Fine, just one little bite—but if I get brainwashed, I'm never trusting you again!"

I took a bite and my whole mouth exploded with flavor. The sandwich was the most amazing combination of taste and texture, as soon as I had the first bite, I had another.

"Pretty great, huh?" Blake asked.

"I'm starting to understand why people line up for this stuff…" I said through a mouthful of sandwich. Okay, so there was no evil magic lurking in the sandwich, just great flavor and amazing bread. Still… it didn't make me any less suspicious of Mistress Bridgette.

Okay, maybe a little bit.

"Where to now then, officer?" I said to Blake.

"There's one more name that came up quite a lot when I was speaking to people the other day, Gwen Garner." Blake finished his sandwich quickly and started the car again.

"Who is she?" I asked.

"Ex-girlfriend of Kaiser Klaus. Apparently, she helped Klaus get his career off the ground, and once he hit the bigtime, he dumped her. Quite a few of Klaus's people said their relationship did not end well."

"Yep, I can imagine why. Where do we find her?"

"According to the computer she runs a women's clothing shop in town. I'm thinking we swing by and pay her a visit."

"Alright, let's hit the road daddio. Do you think we have time to get another sandwich before we leave though?" Blake laughed and pulled back onto the road. "I… I wasn't joking," I mumbled to myself.

BLAKE DROVE BACK across town and pulled up again outside a women's clothing shop named, 'Garner's Garments'. We climbed out of the car and headed towards the shop.

"What are you doing after this?" I asked him.

"Burt wants me to head back to the station and report on my day before I clock out. After that I'll keep an eye on you for a bit and then probably head back to my cabin."

I laughed and shook my head. "You don't have to keep an eye on me, why not just go home and relax? When do you ever take a break?"

"My real job description is quite simple, watch you whenever I can and make sure you don't get killed. I wasn't kidding when I said I was going to pack in this police stuff—I thought it would be a good cover, but it's taking up too much of my time."

"I'm just saying you can have a life outside of protecting me, and look around, I haven't been attacked once today!"

"Now *there's* a way of jinxing things." Blake held open the door for the shop and we both stepped inside. It was a cute little place, but I wasn't sure the clothes were really cut for someone like me. The outfits here were better suited for a high-end businesswoman that stomped around boardrooms. Tight-fitting black dresses and sharp-edged power-suits—I was more a jeans and sneakers kind of gal, maybe a floral dress and cardigan if I was feeling really adventurous.

"Won't be a minute!" a woman called from the back. "Feel free to look around!"

"What do you think?" I said to Blake as I held up a light-grey dress cut to the mid-thigh. "This would look great on you."

"Not my style," he said with a slight smirk. "I'm more of a black or nothing kind of guy."

"Right, sorry about that," the female voice resumed. Looking over I saw a thin blonde woman emerge from the back. "Trying to unpack stock and serving the shop at the same time, always a bit of a—" All of a sudden, she froze upon seeing us, her eyes focused in particular on Blake's police uniform. "Oh, I—you're the police!"

"Correct. Am I right in assuming you are Gwen Garner?"

"T—That's right," she stammered.

"The name is Officer Blake Voss, this here is my associate, Zora Wick. We're—"

Gwen interrupted Blake. "Sorry. Would you excuse me a moment? It's just—I left the iron on, and I can smell something burning. I'll be right back!"

Before Blake could tell her to 'hold it there' the petite blonde disappeared out of sight again. He glanced over at me and spoke in a low voice. "Well, she's acting sketchy as hell."

"You're telling me," I said. "Think she's telling the truth?"

"I've got super senses, and I can't smell burning. Her heart was hammering away like a hummingbird though, and—son of a—the back door!" Blake disappeared through the back of the shop, and I ran after him. My ears couldn't pick up sound like his, but from his reaction alone I could guess that our suspect was making a run for it.

I sprinted through a corridor packed with boxes, into a small kitchen, and stumbled out of the back door and into a rear parking lot just in time to see our suspect peeling away in a bright red sports car. Blake chased her for a few feet before stopping and turning back to see me.

"I could catch her, but I can't use my powers in town, too many humans around."

"It's okay, I'm sure we'll track her down. Still, this is an exciting development, eh?"

"It is?" Blake walked back to me, seemingly confused by my reaction.

"Of course! Why else would she run? Clearly, we have our culprit!"

He pouted as though he hadn't considered it. "You have a way of finding the silver lining, don't you?"

"Blake my dear, one has to see the glass as half full in this type of work. You'd go mad if you didn't. There's an even bigger positive in all of this though."

"What's that?" he asked.

"Now we have time to head back and get another one of those sandwiches!"

Blake groaned. "You are unbelievable."

CHAPTER 15

The weekend, what a wonderful invention. Two full days of lazing around, enjoying the world and going at your own pace for once—unless you're me of course. As the bakery opened on Saturdays it was business as usual. Daphne and I were up at the crack of dawn to get things ready for the day, and with the weekend the real crowds came. We were swept off our feet all morning serving up sugary snacks to Compass Cove's (mostly) delightful inhabitants.

Sunday was the same, with the added caveat that we closed at noon, meaning that we had the entire afternoon to do with as we wanted. "Anything fun planned?" I asked Daphne as we locked up the shop.

"I might go for a swim in the lake, or go and watch a film with my sister..."

"Go to the movies!" I said quickly. "The lake is probably freezing." And full of stark-raving sirens that wanted to snatch humans.

"Yeah, you're right. That new ghost film is out, I think we might go and watch that. What about you?"

"I'm considering having a bath, so I've no doubt my phone will start ringing any second with a problem I need to solve."

Daphne laughed. "Whelp, good luck with that! See you tomorrow!"

I headed upstairs to the apartment and dialed Sabrina from the flamingo phone. As soon as Daphne mentioned the lake I wondered where we were up to with the whole siren snatching problem.

"What's up?" Sabrina said after a few rings. I could barely hear her over an incredibly loud grinding sound in the background.

"Where are you?!" I shouted. "It sounds like you're inside a jet engine!"

The noise died down and Sabrina's voice became clearer. "Sorry, I was making some new wands on the lathe. Is everything okay?"

"Yeah, I'm just wondering if you got in touch with that sea witch."

"I did! I forgot to tell you. She said she can meet tomorrow, but there's one small caveat."

"Here we go, what is it?"

"She needs your help with a spell."

"My help? What on earth could I possibly help her with?!" I could barely magic my way out of a paper bag.

"I sort of let it slip that you're a Prismatic Witch... she got very excited. Sorry, I know we're trying to keep it quiet, but on the plus side this witch literally doesn't talk to anyone apart from me—so it's all good."

"I still don't understand how I can help."

"Well, some spells require different types of magic—so they require multiple witches from different backgrounds. Prismatic Witches are always high in demand because they can switch between magic types easily."

"But I'm still in training wheels, I don't know what I'm doing!"

"Hey, I told *her* that, but she didn't seem to mind. Anyway, once we help her out with this thing, she'll help us track down the sirens."

"Alright, well that seems like a small win. How's your Sunday going?"

"Just working dude. New witches are always coming of age and wands are flying out the door! Not literally, that would be terrible for my stock. Listen, I'll speak to you later, I've got a lot to catch up on. Bye!" Sabrina ended the call.

"You're bored," a voice said from behind me. Turning around I saw my Time Owl, Phoebe, standing inside her cage.

"Am not."

"You are," she noted. "You're looking for something to do."

"Where's Hermes?" I asked. "He's usually up to something mischievous."

Phoebe blinked slowly. "Sorry, can't tell you."

I rolled my eyes and turned away from her. "What help are you?!"

"Hudson," she said.

"What?" As I asked the question my phone started ringing. Sure enough it was Hudson. "I'm not sure how helpful these three second warnings are." I answered the phone. "Yo."

"What did that idiot do now?" he asked.

"That's one heck of a way to start a phone call," I said.

"Blake, what did he do with the Tizzie-Whizzie?"

"The winged hedgehog? I have no idea. What's happened?"

"It's gone. These things don't just up and leave of their own accord, especially when there's still an abundant food source around. You said he tried to take the thing on. It's not in town anymore, so what did he do? I needed to capture that thing, Zora, not set it free!"

"I think Blake gave up on the hedgehog thing. He tried once and it beat the absolute crap out of him—just like it did with you."

"I wouldn't say it beat me up *that* bad. Blake probably got hit a lot worse—his fighting is much more amateur than mine."

"I dunno, you had a broken arm. He had two black eyes. Seems like he got off lighter."

"He's got advanced healing—of course he came out of it looking better! Anyway, this is beside the point. I'm going to have to go and visit him now to find out what he did. Any chance he told you anything? He kind of runs his mouth around you."

"No," I said. "And will the pair of you stop fighting already? You're turning my hairs gray."

"I'll stop fighting when he stops doing stupid things… so never!"

"Real mature. Listen I'm hanging up now, I want to enjoy what's left of my weekend while I still can."

"Hey, I'm getting a Chinese later, want to come with?"

"So I can listen to you complain about Blake for an hour? No thanks." With that I ended the call. I'd barely put the phone down when it started ringing again.

"It's Blake," Phoebe said, almost the exact same time I saw his name on the screen.

"Yeah, thanks," I said sarcastically. I answered the phone. "I swear if this is about Hudson—"

"Hudson? What did that idiot do now?"

I sighed. "*Nothing*. Why are you calling?"

"Yikes, talk about a warm reaction. I just wanted to call and let you know there's still no sign of that Gwen Garner woman. She's vanished into thin air. Looks like she packed up some things at her house and got the heck out of dodge."

"What do we do now then?" I asked.

"Burt has put a statewide notice out for her arrest. She'll get picked up by law enforcement at airports, so she's probably hiding out in a motel in the sticks somewhere. She'll show up soon enough."

"I guess we're kind of sitting on our hands until then, eh?"

"Yeah, I guess so. So entertain me, why did you think I was calling about Hudson?"

"I'd really rather not—"

"I'm just curious!"

"He seems to think you've scared off the flying hedgehog thing."

"What? I told you I wasn't going near that thing again. Besides, I thought he wanted it gone?"

"Yeah, apparently he needed to capture it or something. You really had nothing to do with it?"

"Cross my heart and eat a pie—or however the saying goes. I swear if he comes around here blaming me for his shoddy—"

"I'm going to hang up now," I said.

"Wait!" Blake said quickly. "Do you want to get a pizza or something?"

I almost had to laugh. It was amazing how similar Blake and

Hudson were sometimes. "You know I'd love to, but I don't want to sit and listen to you complaining about your boyfriend for an hour."

"I won't mention him, believe me! The less time I spend talking about that guy the better!"

"Really? Because it seems all that either of you talks about is how much you hate the other. Bye, Blake."

"No, wait—"

I put the phone back in its flamingo cradle as I contemplated what to do with my afternoon. I was half-tempted to sit down and study some magic books, but I couldn't remember the last time I'd actually had a few hours to myself to do nothing, so I decided to sit on the couch and watch some mindless television.

As soon as I picked up the TV remote my phone started ringing again. I looked over at Phoebe. "No warning this time?"

"If you're going to be ungrateful about my abilities then I won't bother!" she said cattily.

"Message received loud and clear," I said wearily. I held up my hand and tried to summon the phone with magic. It zipped through the air and smacked into my forehead. "Son of a—" I moaned. "Hello?"

"Alright, that's enough relaxing for you," Zelda said. "I've got a Sunday afternoon plan for us."

"I think my nose is bleeding." I pinched my nose, my voice sounding all nasal.

"What happened?"

"Tried to summon the phone with magic and hit myself in the face."

"Oh dear, yeah… maybe ease off on the magic until you go to school. Anyway, I know you're probably bored out of your mind, so I thought I'd call."

"I was actually just about sit down and relax in front of the television."

"Forget that, I've got a better plan! Now we've got a minute to ourselves why don't we go to the library and try see what mom was up to!"

"Huh, I'd completely forgot about that actually." I sat up on the couch and pulled my hand away, breathing a sigh of relief as I saw that my nose wasn't bleeding. "It's a Sunday afternoon though, is the library open?"

"The Magical Library is. It's open twenty-four-seven. Even has a coffee shop!"

"Alright, you might have twisted my leg. Where do I meet you, and when?"

"Outside the regular library in half an hour. Be there or be square!"

"Wouldn't miss it for the world…" I muttered.

* * *

THE LIBRARY WASN'T TOO FAR from my apartment, so I decided to walk. It was a rather nice day in Compass Cove, there wasn't a cloud in the sky and the cold winter weather was finally giving way to spring.

When I got there Zelda was already waiting for me outside. The library was a large brownstone building with tall steps and stone columns—it was certainly very official looking. "So how do we get inside?" I asked, looking at a large sign at the bottom of the stairs. The human library was closed on Sundays.

"Follow me!" Zelda said cheerily. "It might look closed, but appearances can be deceiving!"

I followed Zelda up the tall stone steps and watched as she walked right through the closed front doors. Cautiously I placed my hand against the door, and it passed through too. I followed her inside to the library's lobby.

It was a large round room with a detailed plaster ceiling. No one else was around except for an old security guard who was sleeping on a chair. The lobby was a little miniature museum of sorts, with several displays boasting information about Compass Cove's history. Zelda walked over to a display about witches and stopped in front of it. "I tell you what we've got it easy these days," she said. "The things they used to do to our ancestors."

My eyes poured over illustrations of witches being burned at stakes. A few short paragraphs explained how witch hysteria had taken over the town in the late 1800s, leading to the capture and burning of seven different witches.

"Did they really burn these women?" I asked, feeling a little disheartened to see this stuff.

"Oh yes, but it's very unlikely they were witches," Zelda said.

"What do you mean?"

"Think about it, a real witch doesn't have much reason to fear a mob of angry humans. She can use magic to get away. Even a novice witch like yourself can use magical instinct to keep yourself safe. That means that the women they did burn were just ordinary humans, falsely accused of being witches when they weren't."

I leaned in close and read one of the captions. *'On March 15th they did burn the suspected witch, Angela Otto, alleged of witchcraft as her laundry never had creases in it.'* "Blooming heck, they were burning them for any old reason!"

"Yup, it's all a load of nonsense—though I would like to know how that woman never got creases in her laundry."

I found myself entranced by the display case. My eyes in particular were drawn to one picture of a man wearing a long cloak and clutching a bible. *'At the forefront of the witch hunt was the Witch Hunter General— Captain Nathaniel Houlgrave. By his efforts the witches were driven from the area now known as Compass Cove—and after the burning of Elsbeth Collier, Captain Houlgrave declared the witches all destroyed. For his achievements he was recognized by William McKinley, who was president at the time."*

"Jeez, this insanity went all the way to the top!"

"Yup, and there are some people to this day that still have it out for witches. Fortunately, the hysteria has died down a bit since the days of being burned alive. Anyway—we didn't come here for a history lesson." Zelda ran her fingers over the top edge of the display cabinet, tapping three little wooden witches etched into the woodwork. *"Let me in, don't let them see, let me see the witch library."*

All of a sudden, the witch trials display cabinet folded away, revealing a spiral staircase that went down into the ground. I looked over my shoulder at the sleeping security guard, who snorted and shifted slightly in his seat.

"This secret entrance seems very public!" I remarked.

"Nah, it's completely hidden, take a step back," Zelda said. I took a couple of steps back and as I did do it was like a mirage came over the area. The display cabinet was back in its normal position, the staircase completely hidden from sight. I couldn't even see Zelda!

Walking forward again the secret entrance came back into view. "Okay, that's pretty cool."

"Wait until we're inside for real. Follow me!"

CHAPTER 16

Zelda and I descended the spiral staircase for well over a minute. When we finally reached the bottom, we walked through a stone doorway into a huge underground library the likes of which I'd never seen. "This place is massive!" I gasped. Just ahead of us there was a central desk and stemming out like spokes on a wheel were vast bookcases with hundreds and hundreds of shelves. Each shelf was easily the height of a two-story house, and they stretched into the distance without an apparent end.

My sister allowed me a moment to stand there and gawp, as my eyes finally came back to hers, I saw her smiling. "Pretty cool, huh?"

"How have you not brought me here until now?"

"Things can get… pretty weird down here," she said. "I guess I was trying to ease you into the whole witch thing a little. Taking you to the Magic Library on day one is sort of like pushing you into the deep end."

"I mean so far I've dealt with ghosts, werewolves, dark witches, sirens, and a bunch of other weird stuff! I'm not sure anything can surprise me at this point."

Zelda didn't look so sure. "If you say so. Let's get a coffee and then we can ask at the desk about mom and the restricted section. It's just over here, follow me!"

We walked over to the little coffee bar. A few witches were quietly sitting at tables, sipping drinks and reading books. "Wait a second," I said as we approached the bar. A huge grey humanoid figure was working behind the counter. "What is that thing?"

"That 'thing' is called Jerry, and he's a stone golem," Zelda whispered. "Don't make a big deal about it." We stopped in front of the register, and I looked up at the 8ft tall stone giant and gulped. Apart from an apron it wasn't wearing anything. Its face had two hollows for eyes, and a line cut in the rock represented its mouth.

"Zelda!" the booming rock giant said. "Been a while! How you been?"

"Oh, you know me Jerry, just trying to keep my *coal*." Zelda delivered the god-awful pun with a wink. The huge stone golem threw its head back and let out a deep baritone laugh.

"It's been a bit busy back here actually. I was wondering if I could use your assi-stones!" he said back to her.

Zelda joined in the laughter and looked over at me. "Jerry this is my sister, Zora, she's new in town. Could we get two specials?"

"Zelda's sister? Of *quartz* you are. You're practically identical. Nice to meet you!" he boomed.

"Uh... thanks," I said. "Lovely place you have here, I can't *fault* it?"

Again, Jerry's laughter boomed across the library. "I already like her, Zelda. Hold on right there, two specials coming up!"

I watched in fascination as the huge rock golem worked nimbly to get our drinks ready. Once he was finished Zelda paid and we made our way over to the main reception desk.

"So that statue was freaking alive..." I recapped out loud, mostly for my own benefit.

"He's a stone golem, not a statue. Jerry's great, as long as you have a rock-based pun ready for him he'll be your friend for life, plus he makes a pretty great drink."

I took a sip of my drink and was pleasantly surprised. "I agree with that *sediment*, Zelda. Very nice drink!"

"Dude save the puns for Jerry," Zelda said flatly.

"Spoilsport. At least things can't get much weirder than that." Zelda almost did a spit take. "What?"

"Zora that was me easing you into things slowly. You've not met Ethyl yet. She's the head librarian." Zelda led the way over to the main reception desk, a large circular construction with a girl sitting on the other side who couldn't be any older than five.

"How may I help you?" she asked without looking up. A hefty book was open in front of her, it's pages full of mysterious glowing runes.

"Hi Ethyl… how are you doing?" Zelda said in a nervous sing-song voice. I immediately wondered why she was acting so unusual around this little girl.

Upon hearing Zelda's voice 'Ethyl' looked up from her magic book and glared at Zelda. "Zelda Wick!" Ethyl stood up and looked Zelda up and down. "You must be hiding those 37 overdue titles—otherwise I don't see why you'd have any sane reason to step inside here!"

"Oh, good you remembered…" she smiled through her teeth. "I was wondering if I could get an extension?"

"Another extension? They were due back six months ago!" the little girl said, her voice echoing across the library. "I've half a mind to send Jake to come and get them!"

"No!" she said very quickly. I didn't know who Jake was, but Zelda was seemingly terrified of that idea. "No that's not necessary. I'll have the books back to you by the end of the week. I just got carried away!"

"See that you do," Ethyl said and sat back in her chair. For the first time she looked at me and narrowed her eyes. "I know you, you're the one that can't stay out of the newspaper. Zora Wick, the long-lost sister."

It was quite unusual being spoken to like this by such a young girl. I put my hands on my knees and bent down so I was more at her level. "Reading the newspaper is a big thing for your age! Do your mommy and daddy help?"

For a moment the little girl just stared at me with fire in her eyes. She looked at Zelda. "Do me a favor, Wick, if you're going to bring your bonehead relatives here then at least give them a primer before you bring them to me."

I stood up. "Did I do something wrong?"

"I'm 84 years old, cupcake," the little girl said. "So, you can show a little respect. Talk down to me again and I'll whoop your butt so hard you won't sit down for a week!"

"84? But you look so—"

"Young? Yeah, that'll happen when you get hit with an unshakeable age reversing curse. My ex-husband was a very pious man—didn't like cursing at all. I cursed like a sailor, wouldn't stop no matter how hard he tried! He was a bitter little man, and one day he decided he'd had enough. Son of a... *biscuit* hit me with an Unshakeable Curse. Every time I swore it took a week off my life. Took me a while before I'd realized what he'd done!"

"That's terrible," I remarked. "What's an Unshakeable Curse?"

"It's pretty much dark magic," Zelda said. "A wizard or witch permanently sacrifices their magic to afflict someone else with a permanent curse. Nothing can be done to remove it."

"Yikes... talk about vindictive."

"You're preaching to the choir." Ethyl took a bite out of her sandwich. "Now let's get a move on, I've got things to do. What did you two knuckleheads want?"

"We're trying to learn more about our mother," Zelda said. "From what we understand she was one of the only witches in town with access to the restricted section of the library. Is there a chance we could have a temporary pass and see what she was doing back there?"

"Absolutely," Ethyl said.

"Really?!"

"No. You come in here with 37 overdue books and think you can demand the earth? Not a chance in hell!" Ethyl shook her head in disbelief.

"What if we get the books back?" I asked. "Can we have a look then?"

"Absolutely," she said again. Zelda was about to respond with more preemptive excitement when I put my hand over her mouth to stop her. Ethyl chuckled. "Take note Zelda, your sister is clearly the one with the brains. Neither of you are setting foot in the restricted section—I'd rather put a pack of playful otters in charge of the nuclear launch codes."

"Why?" Zelda protested.

"The restricted section is restricted for a reason. The books in there are incredibly dangerous, and only witches and wizards of the highest caliber are allowed inside. Need I remind you what happened to your mother? She had access to the books in there and she disappeared, no small coincidence!"

"We just want to try and find out what might have happened to her —" I began, but Ethyl cut me off again.

"We're done talking here ladies. I won't waste another minute of my time talking to you until I get those overdue books back. If I don't have them by the end of the week, I *will* ban you both."

"But I didn't do anything!" I said.

"Oh, but you did, you made the grave error of being related to this knucklehead! Bring those books back, or you're both banned. Permanently!"

Zelda and I slunk away from the desk with our tails between legs. I'd never been chewed out by a little girl before—the experience was odd to say the least. "Where are we going?" I said as Zelda walked further into the library. "Let's get out of here and grab those books!"

"Ah I'll bring them back tomorrow; I can't be bothered leaving here and coming back. We might as well have a look around while we're here. I can show you a few things at least."

"How big is this place anyway?" I asked as we walked down one of the library's sprawling corridors. The huge bookshelves dwarfed us, and I felt like an ant lost inside a gargantuan structure.

"I don't think anyone really knows. There are magical platforms to help you get around, they move pretty fast though—I always end up feeling travel sick. Is there anything you want to see in particular?"

"Is there a section with any good beginner books on magic? I was hoping to get some prep done before I start school in a few weeks."

"Swatting up, eh?" Zelda said with a grin. "There's an elementary magic section, I think we could find you a good copy of *Blundell's Bumper Book of Beginner Spells*. It's a cornerstone of every young witch's library. Look, there's a platform here, step on."

I stepped onto the wooden platform with Zelda, it wasn't much bigger than a tabletop, with a waist-high rail around the edges and a little wooden gate that Zelda pulled shut. On one side of the railing a curved piece of wood jutted up, and on its face there was a silver moon with eyes and a mouth.

"Where to?" the ornament said, coming to life.

"That thing just talked!" I gasped.

"Wow, talk about rude," the moon-face said. "Do you have a location or what?"

"Beginner books please," Zelda answered. "Ignore her, she's new."

Without warning the platform shot up into the sky. I gripped the railing and let out a small scream as it took off into the library. Bookshelves blurred past us at rapid speed while the platform flew around corners. A few moments later it set us down again in an entirely different section. The little wooden gate flew open, and the platform made a jerking motion to throw us off. "Come on, I haven't got all day!" it said before flying off again.

"That might just be the rudest magical platform I've ever met," I said as I brushed myself off.

"They're all pretty short. That one was quite pleasant as far as they go. Come on, beginner books are right over here."

Zelda spent a good half hour showing me around some beginner books. In the end I only ended up taking one, the beginner book of spells she had mentioned on the way here. "Is Ethyl even going to let me take a book out? She was just threatening to ban us for life," I noted.

"Do you know how many times I've been permanently banned from this library? Ethyl is all bark an no bite, we'll be fine, trust me."

"Check Zelda out with the rebellious streak. I never thought I'd see you breaking rules."

"Please Zora, you're looking at one of Compass Cove's rare

members of the Emerald-level Bookworm club. I don't want to brag, but I'm a pretty big deal around here—the library is my domain."

"Wow, I never realized I was in the presence of celebrity," I said sarcastically. "How does one reach emerald-level? Read a lot of books?"

"Well yes, but when you put it that way it doesn't sound impressive. There's actually a lot more to it," Zelda said defensively.

"Really, like what?"

"I don't have the time to explain it to you—a non-bookworm wouldn't understand."

"Yes, I'm sure it's all very complicated. Shall we get out of here then? I need to start thinking about dinner."

We found another magical platform and Zelda asked to be taken back to the library's central desk. "A little slower this time," she asked. "I nearly threw up on the last ride."

"Wuss!" the magical moon-face said.

Once again, the platform took off, albeit a little slower. A few minutes into the ride an idea occurred to me. "Say, Zelda, it sounds like being an emerald-level bookworm is a pretty big deal."

"Yes, I thought I already made that clear. So what?"

"Well I'm just wondering, shouldn't someone of your status have automatic access to the restricted section? It kind of goes without saying really."

Zelda opened and closed her mouth as she tried to think of a response. Clearly she didn't want to lose face and admit she couldn't do whatever she liked, but I knew her ego wouldn't let her. "Probably, but like you said it's time to go home anyway. I'm getting hungry too."

"Ah, what's one more stop?" I said to her. I looked at the little moon-face. "Change of direction, take us to the forbidden section."

The moon-faced ornament just laughed at me. "Like I'm going to let a couple of amateurs like yourself into the restricted section! Think again!"

"Now listen here you rude little—" I'd had just about enough of the rude platforms and jabbed my finger at the talking metallic face. As I did something strange happened, a multi-colored stream of light erupted from my finger and trickled over the platform.

"Restricted section, coming right up!" the platform said in a much cheerier voice, one that sounded a little hypnotized.

"What did you do?!" Zelda hissed. "You messed it up with your magic!"

"I just poked it; I didn't do anything!"

"Well make it stop, we can't actually go to the restricted section!"

"Stop!" I said, poking the face over and over. "Stop, stop!"

The platform was oblivious though, it took a sharp corner, and the turn nearly threw us out. We both crouched low and clung on for dear life. A minute later the flying platform approached a set of tall black doors that were almost as big as a full-sized church. We passed through a small opening near the top of the doors, and on the other side we found ourselves in a dark and gloomy chamber full of shadowy bookcases. The platform set down on the mist-covered floor and threw us off. "Later!" it sang and roared away.

"Well now you've gone and done it," Zelda said in a frantic whisper. "We're trapped in the restricted section and we're going to die!"

"We'll be fine, let's just get out of here—unless you want to do some poking around?"

"What are we even looking for you idiot? We have no idea what mom was doing in here!"

"...That's a very good point. I guess we rushed into this without a plan."

"We?! This has nothing to do with me!" Zelda hissed. "This is all you and your dangerous finger jabbing!"

"Will you chill out already? It was a mistake. I don't know what happened. Let's just—"

Just then I heard a huge thud in the mist behind us. Turning around I saw the silhouette of a tall figure walking towards us. Zelda and I both grabbed hold of one another, trembling as the huge creature approached. A set of red glowing eyes illuminated.

"Zelda, what do we do?!" I whispered.

"I don't know, I don't know!" she repeated over and over.

The figure emerged from the mist, a ten-foot-tall humanoid wearing Egyptian looking armor with a Jackal head. "Is that one of those Ancient Egyptian pyramid guards?" I said, feeling utterly confused.

"That's Jake, the library security guard. He's Ethyl's lapdog!"

The large Anubis knelt down before us, held out its golden hands and placed them on both of our shoulders. As soon as it did, we teleported back to the library's main desk. Ethyl was waiting for us, her hands on her hips.

"Really? Breaking into the forbidden section? I really expected more of an Emerald-level bookworm like you, Zelda Wick!" she roared with indignation. "I'm afraid you leave me with no other choice, you are both permanently banned from Compass Cove Magical Library!"

"No!" Zelda wailed. "It was a mistake!"

"The only mistake here was me letting you back in. You've been towing the line for a long time, and your sister clearly isn't any better. Go on, get out of here. You're banned with immediate effect! If I see you in here again there will be hell to pay!"

Ethyl snatched the book of beginner magic from my hand and her large jackal-headed guard silently escorted us to the spiral staircase.

"Well, look on the bright side, that could have gone worse," I said as we left the library.

"How could that have possibly gone worse?!" Zelda flustered.

"We could have died. And the trip wasn't completely wasted, we learned something."

"Yeah, never go anywhere with you again."

"Not quite," I said as we walked down the tall stone steps. "My magic can get us inside the restricted section. We might be banned, but we *do* have a way of getting in there."

Zelda just shook her head. "You know I thought I should book another appointment with Doctor Yamgov, but I have no doubt about it now. You are out of your mind!"

I punched Zelda on the arm softly and grinned to try and cheer her up. "It's genetic, remember? If I'm crazy, then you're crazy too. We're all losing our marbles around here."

"That would explain why I keep hanging around with you!" she shrieked.

CHAPTER 17

The library may have been a complete disaster, but I was still certain that Zelda and I would be able to get back in there once she returned her books. Ending up in the restricted section was an accident after all, and I was sure Ethyl had it in her heart to forgive us—maybe.

Monday morning came around and Daphne and I had a busy time serving customers. At some points there was even a line out of the door! Just after lunchtime I got a call from Sabrina, letting me know our meeting with the sea witch was still on.

"Good news, Mira has given me the greenlight. Come on over and I'll take you to her place!"

"Right now? I'm just getting ready for the afternoon rush."

"Well that's what you hired Daphne for, isn't it? Mira doesn't invite people around often Zora. If you want to solve this siren problem, then I'd act fast!"

"Alright, stay calm. I'll be there in a few minutes." I hung up the phone and came into the front to speak to Daphne. "So—"

"It's fine." She looked back at me and laughed. "Just go dude, you're the boss, you don't need to explain it to me!"

"I *do* sometimes work full days in here, I promise. Are you okay to lockup? I don't know how long this is going to take."

"I think I can take care of it. I'll take the keys back to my place, just call around when you're done."

"Thanks Daphne, I owe you like a million by this point."

I headed out to the garage behind the shop so I could get the van. I had just opened the doors when I heard a metallic clang from my right. Looking over I saw a man squeezing out of the drainpipe, it was Clarence Hogman, the Wand Insurance salesman. "Zora Wick, just the person I wanted to see!" he said as he pushed himself up onto his feet.

"Listen dude I'm *really* busy—"

"I'm just dropping in because I never got that call from you. Now I know, *I know*, you're a modern woman—you've got boardroom meetings and homeowners associations to deal with, but ask yourself this —what price do you put on your own personal protection?"

I let out a flustered breath. "Let's skip the jargon, I spoke to my friends—it's not illegal to pass on Wand Insurance. You lied to me."

"I did nothing of the sort!" he said, looking gravely offended. "All I said is that the Wand Insurance Group have advisory laws, and they strongly advocate that all wand users have wand insurance!"

"Of course, *they* do!" I said, throwing my hands into the air. "If you were selling umbrellas, you'd tell people it's about to rain!"

"Miss Wick I think you're confused," Clarence chuckled. "I'm selling *wand insurance,* not umbrellas—"

"Have you ever heard of a metaphor?" I asked. "Listen Clarence, the fact of the matter is that you lied to me. I don't need the insurance, and my cousin makes wands. If this one breaks I think I'm fine, I don't need your overpriced insurance to sleep at night!"

Clarence stared at me for a long moment and then he nodded. "If that's really how you feel."

"I'm sorry for shouting, I just have a really important meeting to get to. I know you're just doing a job, but can you... can you just leave me alone?" I started walking towards the van when Clarence cleared his throat.

"Well..." he began.

I turned on my heels. "What is it now?"

"Due to regulations and laws I'm legally allowed to visit you sixteen times before I have to respectfully cease all contact."

I blinked, unable to believe what I was hearing. "Someone's really lobbying hard for the Wand Insurance group, eh?"

"Ain't that the truth! Look, I have sales targets, and if I don't follow up on my appointments, I'll lose my job. I've got kids! I can't get canned Miss Wick. Luckily I think there's an arrangement that might just satisfy us both."

"And what's that?" I said flatly.

"It's a limited time deal. You take out a free one-month trial on our most premium insurance package and I don't have to visit you anymore! You can cancel before the billing period starts and I'll even get a little commission. You'll also get a few weeks of premium insurance protection for absolutely nothing! Your wand so much as snaps and – poof! – I will personally show up in seconds to bring you a new one! We'll also throw in a free magic boost, free of charge!"

"So I cancel this thing before the end of the month and I don't lose a dime?" I clarified.

"I swear on my mothers' Pontiac Firebird," Clarence said and crossed his heart. "All I need to know is your wand type and your card details."

"I'm a Prismatic Witch," I said. Clarence's eyes nearly bugged out of his skull as he heard the words.

"Oh boy, don't meet one of them every day! No worry though, we can still insure that. I'd actually recommend you settle for nothing less than our premium service for a rare case like this…let me get the paperwork together really quickly!"

A few minutes later I'd dotted the i's and crossed the t's. "If I somehow get ripped off during all this, I will teleport you to the moon," I threatened. Clarence looked a little apprehensive. Ever since I'd dropped the 'Prismatic' word he almost seemed afraid of me.

"Can you do that?" he gulped. "I mean I heard witches like you are powerful, but I—"

"I'm just kidding. Now I hope you take no offense to this Clarence, but do I ever have to see you again?"

Clarence packed away his things and shook my hand. "No siree, ma'am! An no offense taken, that's not the first time someone's asked me that question. Enjoy your day now!"

The wand insurance salesman squeezed back into the drainpipe, vanishing in his mysterious way. "I really should have asked him about the strange entrance thing," I muttered to myself.

Fifteen minutes later I pulled up outside Sabrina's shop and headed inside. Her shop sold all sorts of magical oddities, and everywhere you looked there was clutter and chaos—the kind that made you want to stay and browse for hours. "Sabrina?" I called. "Where are you?!"

I heard a distant grinding sound coming from underneath my feet and realized she must have been in her workshop. She did mention that she made wands in the basement.

Through an open door behind the counter I saw flashes of light, as I reached the door I found stairs leading down and I followed them. They opened into a basement, in the middle of which was a huge machine that almost looked like a giant gun, it was spinning in all directions, belching flashes of light and loud metallic banging sounds. Sitting squat in the middle was Sabrina, wearing a black pair of goggles and holding onto a pair of handles for dear life.

She saw me enter and shouted something, but I could barely hear her over the din. Every few seconds another flash of magical colorful light filled the room and left an afterimage on the back of my eyes. Plumes of smoke jettisoned in all directions and the entire basement shook around the machine.

"Nearly finished!" I heard her shout before the machine grew even louder. It concluded its erratic mechanical ballet with one final bang and then settled down, joints hissing and letting out steam. Sabrina hopped out of the machine's cockpit and thrust her fist into the air. "Pretty awesome, huh?!" she shouted—she pulled out some earplugs. "Oops, sorry, didn't realize I was shouting."

"You were making a wand just now?" I asked in amazement.

"Yeah, it's a chaotic affair, eh? Let's check out the final result." Sabrina walked over to a small compartment at the very front of the machine and unlocked a metal door. She put on an oven mitt and pulled out a smoking stick not much bigger than a pen. "A fantastic wand for a kitchen witch," she said. "This baby will fetch a premium."

"If you say so." I knew next to nothing about wands or how they were valued. "I actually just got wand insurance would you believe..."

Sabrina groaned. "Finally wore you down, did they?" She laughed. "Yeah, they're pretty tenacious. Give me a minute to get all my gear off and then we can head to Mira's. I'll meet you upstairs."

I headed back up and momentarily lost myself as I explored the fascinating aisles of Sabrina's shop. Although wands were her strong suit, she sold all sorts of interesting things, most of which I had no idea what they did. I walked past a grandfather clock that had a portrait of an old man in it. "Want to know how you die?" he asked.

"Shut up, Edgar," Sabrina said as she came upstairs. I had pivoted on my heels to regard the creepy clock.

"Did he really just say that?"

"Yeah, it's cursed, I think. Bought it at a magical auction out of town a few weeks ago, and it seemed fine at the time. He's always saying really creepy things though—the seller said I could send it back for a refund, I just haven't had a moment to pack him up."

"The blood moon is coming; the shadow of the ends time is upon us all!" the creepy clock said again.

"If you don't shove a sock in it, you're going straight in the wood-chipper!" Sabrina threatened.

"Alright, I was just joking!" the old man in the painting said.

"Come on, let's get to Mira's place."

'Mira's place' was far east out of town, heading in the direction of Eureka, the town on the eastern coast of Compass Cove lake. Until recently the roads had been completely washed out thanks to a small earthquake, but Sheriff Burt and his boys had been cleaning up the roads, and for the first time since moving here I could actually drive there.

We were only passing through apparently, because Mira's place was outside of Eureka even, but as I glanced the town, I saw smart buildings that looked all business and academic. "Of the four towns around the lake Eureka is the brainiac one. Everyone here is a professor, a lawyer, a tech-geek or a scientist of some sort. The town was founded as a 'beacon of intellectual hope'," Sabrina explained as she saw me eye the passing town.

"I guess we should pass through quickly then," I joked.

"You're kidding, but there are plenty of snobs around here."

We passed through town and the road became a gravel track that wound over the hills and down toward the coast. It ended at a lighthouse set upon a mound of craggy rock. For the first time since moving here I saw the Atlantic ocean, its great waves smashing against the rocky coast and exploding in clouds of white mist. Somewhere to my south a culvert of water connected this ocean to Compass Cove 'lake'.

"Is this lighthouse the home of our sea witch?" I asked Sabrina.

"Sure is!"

We parked up outside the lighthouse and walked towards the door. All around us the sound of crashing waves permeated the air. Sabrina knocked on the door and it opened a crack, revealing two almond shape eyes and a mass of tangled black hair.

"This her?" the woman hiding on the other side of the door said in a quiet voice.

"Hi Mira, this is my cousin, Zora."

Mira opened the door, revealing a small Asian woman swamped in an oversized knit jumper. "Come in then, quickly!" she said. Sabrina and I slipped inside, and Mira shut the door behind us.

"Nice place you got here," I said, looking around at the messy lighthouse interior.

"I spend most of my time outside," Mira answered. "Let's get to work then, over here!"

We followed her up a metal staircase to the first floor, where a cauldron was bubbling away and letting off flashes of purple light. A large spell book was open on a stand next to the cauldron.

"I'm not the most experienced witch," I began, eager to set the record straight before I embarrassed myself.

"Doesn't matter, just need your unique aura, put your hands on the cauldron." Mira apparently wasn't much for eye contact or small talk. She went over to her spell book and started reading. I glanced at Sabrina to check this was normal, a nod indicated that *maybe* it was?

I put my hands on the metal and a surge of power swept through the cauldron. "What is the spell for anyway?" I asked Mira.

"It's an ascension spell, I'm moving to the next level of my magic. A Prismatic witch is needed for such a ritual. To be honest I never thought I'd meet one."

"Is it… safe?"

"For you? Perfectly so. The change will only come over me."

"Ascension is dangerous Mira, you know that right?" Sabrina clarified. "There's a reason people don't do it much anymore—not just because it's hard to do."

"Don't worry Sabrina, I've been waiting to do this for a long time. Once it's done, I'll be able to breathe under water, talk with sea creatures and walk upon the waves. My work will be a lot easier to do!"

A rising tide of pressure swelled throughout the room as Mira worked through the ritual. As she reached the final magical declaration and explosion of wind ripped through the small room and the light in the cauldron went out. Sabrina and I stayed in place, but Mira blasted backwards, smashed into a wall and collapsed against the ground. We both ran over to her and helped her up.

"I'm fine!' she said joyously. As we picked her up, I realized her skin was glowing with golden light. It faded after a moment, and she returned to normal. "The ritual was a success, thank you Zora."

"No problem," I muttered. "Just kind of held my hands on a cauldron."

"And now you fulfill our end of the bargain," Sabrina said as she helped Mira to her feet. "How do we find the merfolk that have moved onto the land?"

"Cody, Aria!" Mira shouted, lifting her head to look upstairs. Suddenly two figures came down the steps, wrapped in moth-eaten clothes that looked like they'd come out of a charity shop. Though they both looked human, from their sharp-featured faces I could tell these were the missing sirens.

"You're the ones that left?" I asked. The boy nodded.

"That's right, and we're not going back. It will take some time adjusting to life on the land, but we can't live down there anymore. Life under Edra has become unbearable!"

Mira stepped forward. "They both came to me a few weeks ago and expressed their desire to leave the water permanently. I have housed them here ever since."

"Why leave?" Sabrina asked. "Why now? Your queen wants our cousin, and her friend. She wants to take them to depths and convert them!"

"That sounds fitting with her madness," the girl said. "Edra wasn't always like this, but recently her mind has gone to the shallows."

"She's asked that we bring you back," I asked. "Only then will our friends be free to return to land."

"We will never return," the boy said defiantly. "Not while Edra wallows in her madness. The others see it too, but they're all afraid to do anything about it."

"They say the change came about recently," Mira said. "As though she's possessed by something."

"Aria has a theory," Cody said. "Tell them."

The girl looked sheepish, but she did speak up after some encouragement. "We had visitors recently, witches. They came bringing tribute."

"Witches?" I asked. "What did they want?"

"They said they didn't want anything, they just wanted to show their appreciation. Edra was ecstatic, and the tribute they brought was very valuable. A black pearl necklace imbued with silver and blue sapphire—there can't be another necklace like it in the whole ocean."

"I recall seeing that around your queen's throat."

Cody nodded. "She hasn't taken it off since putting it on, and ever since she put it on, she changed! We think the tribute was cursed, it's poisoning her mind and our tribe! You need to help us. Destroy it and save our people!"

"What did these witches look like?" Sabrina asked.

"They wore dark cloaks and hoods over their faces," Aria answered. "Human faces are difficult to remember for our kind, but their features were shrouded with shadow."

"Sound like anyone you know?" I said, looking at Sabrina.

"You think this is The Sisters of the Shade?" she gasped.

"They fit the description; don't you think?"

The Sisters of the Shade were a group of dark witches hell-bent on converting me to the dark side and taking control of Compass Cove. Magical barriers supposedly prevented the dark witches from entering our territory, but it seemed they had somehow slipped through the cracks.

"We won't go back to Edra," Cody reiterated. "Not while she acts this way!"

I considered their words for a moment and listened to the rhythmic crashing of the ocean waves outside. Finally, I nodded as I came to a conclusion. "Very well, I'm not going to drag you back to your tribe—especially if what you say is true."

Both of the human-sirens breathed a sigh of relief.

"Zora?" Sabrina said with confusion. "We can't just leave them here! You heard what the merfolk said, if we don't return their lost members then Celeste and Gordo are gone!"

"Relax, they're not taking anyone. Clearly the Sisters of the Shade are trying to stir up trouble here, so we'll have to right their wrongs. We're going to destroy the necklace poisoning Edra's mind." I looked at Cody and Aria. "I have the beginnings of a plan, and I think it will have to involve you. Can I rely on you? I'll need a day or two to put things together."

"You really think you can fix things?" Aria asked with concern.

"I can but try. If things come to the worst, I'll probably die at the hand of a mad siren queen." Just another regular sentence that came out of my mouth these days.

CHAPTER 18

"Wait, which one is which again?" Daphne asked while handing a customer their change the next morning.

"Blake is a werewolf cop, Hudson works for this... actually I can't tell you that bit. But they've both assigned themselves as my guardians and they hate each other. It would be funny if they weren't so annoying. Also they show up all the time—they both practically stalk me."

"I wish two superhot dudes would stalk me," Daphne pouted. "My last boyfriend used to steal money from my purse."

Just then I saw Blake through the front window of the shop. "Speak of the devil," I said. "This one is Blake."

"Morning ladies," Blake said heartily as he came through the front door. "How are we doing on this fine Monday morning?"

"Pretty normal. Why are you so chipper?" I asked.

"I was hoping you might ask that." Blake came up to the counter and pointed at a doughnut with chocolate frosting. "One of those please," he said to Daphne. He looked at me again and smiled.

"Okay this is very weird, even for you. Are you going to tell me what's going on?"

"A state trooper arrested a woman checking into a motel last night. Three hours outside of Compass Cove."

"Gwen Garner?" I asked with excitement. Several days had passed since our third suspect in the Kaiser Klaus case had disappeared into the sunset in her bright red sportscar.

"The one and only. She'll be at the station in a few minutes, I came over to see if you wanted to help me interview her?"

"Does a one-legged duck swim in circles?" I asked.

"What happened to the duck's other leg?" he asked with a note of fake concern.

"Has no one in this town heard of rhetorical questions? Let me take my apron off and get my things, I'll be with you in five minutes."

I BUCKLED myself into the cruiser and Blake pulled out onto the main street. "I noticed you were doing more siren hunting yesterday. How did that go?"

"How exactly do you always know what I'm up to?" I asked. "Do you have a magic mirror or something?"

Blake smirked. "A good magician never reveals his secrets."

"Were you following me yesterday?"

"For a little bit, I figured you were safe enough for the most part. Can't believe you bought that wand insurance by the way."

"I'm thinking we both set up boundaries. Are you familiar with that word?"

"I am, unfortunately that idea directly contradicts the responsibilities bestowed upon me as your keeper." Blake shot a big grin my way. I just rolled my eyes and looked out the window. "So, how did it go?" he prompted.

"Eh, not bad. I *found* the sirens at least, they're hiding out with a sea witch."

"Why did they leave the water in the first place?"

I explained the events so far to Blake, and how the runaway merfolk suspected that their queen had been cursed by The Sisters of the Shade. "So yeah, it looks like they're still a problem. I thought they weren't able to get inside the town boundaries?"

"So did I, but that's the thing about evil folk, they'll always find a way to get in. You know it seems this town is rife with cursed items. First the ring on our murder victim's finger, and now this necklace on the siren queen."

"You think they're connected somehow?" I asked.

"I'm not sure, seems a bit coincidental though, doesn't it?"

"You know now that you mention it, I was at Sabrina's yesterday and she said she'd accidentally bought a few cursed items from a vendor." I watched the town pass by for a moment as Blake continued to drive. "Are cursed items common in the magical world?"

"I mean I'm not super involved with witch culture, but I don't think cursed items are *this* common. We have eyewitness accounts that these dark witches gave a cursed necklace to the merfolk, I wouldn't be surprised if they're behind the other items too."

My grandmother Liza warned me that the Sisters of the Shade would resort to tactics like this. Was it possible they were deliberately flooding the town with cursed items to try and spread chaos? It certainly seemed like the sort of thing they would do.

A few moments later Blake pulled into the parking lot outside the police station, and we headed inside. Linda, Burt's wife and the acting receptionist, gave a hearty welcome as we came in.

"If it isn't my favorite amateur detective!" she said. "Blake honey they just brought her in, she's in the back."

"Awesome. Let's go check it out, Zora."

"Officer Voss I was hoping I might have a moment with Miss Wick?"

Blake turned and shrugged. "Sure. I'll wait for you at my desk, Zora." Blake left and I turned to look at Linda. The woman was a crossword enthusiast, and she only ever wanted to talk to me when she was stuck.

"This better not be about—" I began.

"Six letters, raggedly dressed city child," she said over me.

"I'm not doing this anymore; I have a reason to be here! A suspect is in waiting, and I'm here to interview them!"

Linda closed her puzzle book and stared at me. "Miss Wick I'm afraid if you do not cooperate, I'll have to ask you to leave this police station! A civilian like yourself can't just wonder around here without the explicit permission of a law enforcement officer!"

"You're seriously making me do this," I groaned.

"Come on, help me! I've been stuck on this for two hours!"

"Really? Because it's obvious. It's *urchin.*"

Linda's face lit up like a Christmas tree. "Ooh, I knew you would get it! Go right in, you never disappoint, Wick!"

I made my way over to Blake's desk. "Everything alright back there?" he asked and stood up from his desk.

"Oh yes, just a terribly important talk. Nothing asinine at all. Let's go interview this suspect, eh?"

We made our way into the interview room and found Gwen Garner sitting at the table in handcuffs. It looked like she hadn't slept well in the few days she'd been on the run. "How was your road trip?" Blake grinned. Gwen Garner didn't seem to appreciate the joke.

"Can I get a coffee?" she asked. "Black, no sugar, no milk or creamer!"

Blake sighed; he was just about to sit down. "Fine. I'll get a drink. Zora, you want anything?"

"Nah, I'm good."

"So, running from the police—that's always a bold decision," I said as I joined Gwen at the table.

"I freaked out, okay? I've never been in trouble before. I already know I'm not getting out of this one—so I made the wrong choice and panicked!"

Blake came back in with two drinks and sat down at the table. "Okay, let's start talking then. What would you like to tell us?"

Gwen took a long sip of her drink and brushed her hair out of her face before taking a deep breath. "My accountant said it was all legal. He was always very particular about the language he used. It's not *evasion,* it's *avoidance.* It's not *illegal,* it's a *legal loophole.* I'll admit I had a funny feeling that it was all too good to be true, I guess I knew it would all catch up to me at some point. It was the holiday to Hawaii, wasn't it? I knew I was pushing my luck putting it down as an expense. I go and book it and then you show up at my door. I mean I should have known—" Gwen paused, realizing that Blake and I both looked *very* confused. "Wait, why are you both looking at me like that?"

"Let's rewind a couple steps here," I said. "We walked into your shop the other day to talk to you. I'm just realizing now that you bolted before Officer Blake here could tell you *what* our business was."

Gwen looked confused now as well. "Wait a second, you're telling me this isn't about the taxes?"

"Uh..." Blake said, drawing the sound out over a very long syllable. "Taxes? You seriously went on the run because you thought this was about taxes?"

Gwen Garner sat up straight, her eyes white with fear. "Uh... ignore everything I just said," she laughed nervously. "I was joking of course. I know what you want to talk about."

"Please," I said. "Indulge me. Why are we sitting here?"

"You wanted to talk about... unpaid parking tickets?" she guessed.

Blake leaned forward to. "I'm sorry, are you seriously telling me—" I put my hand on Blake's shoulder.

"Hold on a second, let's talk outside quickly." We both got up from the table and left the room.

"Are you hearing this? She ran away because she thinks she's in tax trouble?!" Blake said in a low whisper.

"Yeah, I don't know what to think. Either she's genuinely oblivious, or she's trying to play ignorant. She's certainly had a day or two to try and come up with this plan. I guess we'll just have to ask questions and see what we learn."

We headed back inside and joined Gwen at the table again. "Did I say something wrong?" she asked.

"If you don't know then we'll just come out and say it." Blake put his hands on the table. "This isn't about tax evasion or unpaid parking tickets... though I *will* have to report that. We're working a murder investigation. We're trying to find out who killed Kaiser Klaus."

"Kaiser?" Gwen gasped, tears immediately brimming in her eyes. "He's... he's dead? How?!"

"You seriously haven't heard anything about this?" Blake asked.

"He's not been part of my life for years, how could I—why would I —how did he die?!"

"Knife to the back," I said. "We discovered the body in his dressing room at the convention. His hands and feet were bound."

Gwen started sobbing wildly, her entire face turning red and blotchy. She buried her head in her cuffed hands as she broke down. It was deeply uncomfortable, but as I looked over at Blake, I saw a man about to crawl out of his skin.

"I'll uh… get some tissues?" he asked with uncertainty. He disappeared out of the room, leaving the two of us alone.

"You really didn't know," I said, more as a statement than a question. Gwen took a huge breath to try and compose herself, fanning her face with her hands to quell the tears.

"I mean I knew he was back in town, but I made no attempt to check in with him. Things ended between us years ago. He's not a part of my life anymore!"

Blake came back in with the tissues and Gwen took them gratefully. It was about ten minutes until she finally composed herself to the point of being able to talk. She wiped at the dark makeup streaks under her eyes and took another huge breath.

"Okay, sorry about that. Let's do this then. What did you want to know?"

"You're sure you're okay?" Blake confirmed.

"I mean I wasn't expecting any of *this*, but I suppose it's happening now. Do you have suspects? Any idea who'd do this?"

"We've spoken with a few people, but so far we have no leads."

Something occurred to Gwen then. "Oh god, you think I did this? And I ran as well! Oh Gwen, you idiot!"

Blake pushed his chair back and leaned forward. "Look, I'm not going to lie to you miss, you *are* a suspect. On the day of Kaiser Klaus' death I spoke with several different people in his entourage and more than one named you as a person of interest."

"Me? Kaiser and I broke up years ago!"

"How did your relationship come to an end?" I asked. "Was it amicable?"

Gwen scoffed. "That's not the word I would use. I started off as Kaiser's personal assistant. I was there from the very beginning. Eventually I ended up being his agent—I helped turn him into a household name. I don't think he'd be where he is today without me."

"So where did everything go wrong?" Blake said.

"Things were going really well for us, or Kaiser, should I say. It was clear that his career was about to take off and he was going to hit the bigtime—right before that happened, he came into my office and told me it was over. He told me to get out immediately and that things were over between us. He even withheld a big bonus that was coming my way."

Blake gave me a knowing look. We'd heard this story once before. It seemed that Kaiser had a history of screwing his employees over.

"How did you react?" I asked.

"I was devastated, naturally. Before that moment he'd given no hint of ending things between us. I was devoted to him, I worked myself to the bone for years, and once it all came to fruition… he threw me to the curb like I was nothing. I tried to find out what had gone wrong, but he cut all contact—he turned into a ghost. So, I decided to take the hint and I never tried to contact him again."

"When did you last see him?" Blake asked.

"It's literally been years. I have no interest in checking in, even though he does come to town once a year. Do you know I can't even eat bread now without feeling sick? He really messed me up." Gwen took a sip of her drink, made a funny face and put the cup down. "Is there sugar in this? I specifically asked for no sugar."

"I might have got the drinks mixed up, sorry," Blake said and glanced down at his own black coffee. "I thought this tasted a little bitter."

Gwen looked like she was about to have a minor breakdown. "I literally haven't eaten a gram of sugar in four years, this is how I fall off the wagon?!"

"My apologies," Blake said. "I'll go and get you another drink." Once again Blake got up and left the room.

"Four years? Talk about a hardcore diet," I joked.

"Diet? Nothing of the sort. I'm a sugar addict in recovery."

"Ah, I'm still deep... deep in that hole. I even run a bakery," I admitted.

"So, you're part of the problem. Profiting off the most addictive drug in our country. I hope you don't sell to kids."

"Are we still talking about sugar here?" I asked, starting to feel a little confused.

"The nation's sugar addiction is an unseen crisis! Do you know how much I used to weigh? I was three-hundred pounds. I'm one-twenty now!"

Sitting across the table from me Gwen looked all skin and bones. It looked like she had swapped one eating problem for another. "Quite the achievement, congratulations. Kicking sugar must have been hard. How did you do it?"

"Pfft, just about any and every distraction you can think of! Knitting little jumpers for my cat—tried that as a side business for a while—didn't pan out. I even joined a sailing club, but I couldn't get my head around the darn knots. They kicked me out after a week."

Blake came back in with Gwen's sugar-free black coffee. "Alrighty, let's get back to things. Where were you on the day of the bread fair?"

"I was working in my clothing shop. I don't mean to brag, but I've made quite a success of myself over these past few years. I'm in there basically every free hour I've got. There are cameras, I can back that statement up!"

"You weren't tempted to go and pay Kaiser a visit at the Bread Fair?" Blake asked.

Gwen sipped her coffee and shook her head emphatically. "Are you kidding me? Getting dumped by Kaiser was the best thing that ever happened to me—I wasn't kidding when I said we'd been no contact. I was devastated at first, but with time I came to realize that he was a spiteful and mean little man."

Although I'd already drawn my own conclusions about Gwen there was one last question I wanted to ask. "You were awfully choked up when we told you about Kaiser's passing. Considering there's so much animosity between you two... I wouldn't have expected such an emotional reaction."

"I mean he meant something to me once upon a time. Things ended badly between us, yes, but we still had good times together. I might not look it, but I *am* quite an emotional person."

I stared at her for a long moment and then looked over to Blake. "I think we're done here."

"Wait, really?" he asked with surprise.

"Yeah, you can let her go—she's telling the truth."

I got up and left the interview room, Blake following closely behind. He caught up to me in the hallway. "Are you sure? We barely asked her anything!"

"She told me everything I need to know. I'll go over it with you later."

"It's Zelda's afternoon off today. If I hurry over to her place, I might be able to get us back into the library."

Blake nodded, but he looked a little defeated. "Three suspects down, what do we do now? The investigation is at a dead end!"

"I don't know," I said, but I felt the same way. "Usually I find the best thing to do when you hit a dead end is turn around and head back in the opposite direction."

"What's that supposed to mean?!" Blake called after me as I walked down the hallway.

"Take a break or something, you'll figure it out!"

CHAPTER 19

"Where in the name of Jason Mamoa have you been?" I said, mouth agape as Hermes strolled into the kitchen the following morning. He looked around as if there was someone else I'd be talking to.

"Me?" he asked.

"Yeah, you! I haven't seen you for two days, where have you been?"

"Taking care of business," he said through a fiendish grin. "I bet you want to know, don't you?"

"That depends, have you caused a problem?" I took a bite of my toast and washed it down with some tea. Hermes looked horribly offended by the question.

"I beg your pardon? Me? Cause a problem? I'll have you know I was making *your* life easier! But I guess if that's the attitude you're going to give me—"

I rolled my eyes as Hermes dialed the melodrama up to 11. "Alright take it easy Mariah Furry."

Hermes stopped, and his mouth dropped open with my pun. "You know I was about to be in a mood with you, but 'Mariah Furry' is genius. I mean I *was* acting like a diva, and I'm covered in fur—really Zora, sometimes your pun work is quite inspired."

"A thank you, a thank you," I said, waving my hands through the air like an opera singer as they drank in applause. "But really, come over here and tell me what you've been up to. I have to admit I'm curious!"

"Constance—" Phoebe said suddenly from her cage. We both turned and looked at the owl. I eyed my phone on the table for a second, but Constance couldn't use phones on account of being a ghost—so *that* didn't make any sense.

"What about her?" I asked.

"Kitchen table in ten seconds. With a friend as well."

It took me a moment to realize what Phoebe was trying to tell me. "She's going to pop through the table?" I pushed my chair back and sure enough Constance popped through the woodwork a moment later.

"Boo!" she said, beaming at me devilishly. Thanks to Phoebe's warning it was the first time Constance had popped up without scaring me. She noted the lack of reaction and pouted. "Oh no fair. You didn't jump! I must be losing my touch."

Constance floated up through the table and plonked herself on one of the kitchen counters. I looked through her transparent blue figure at Phoebe. "Now *that's* the kind of foresight I find useful! Nice work Phoebe." The time owl ruffled her feathers slightly. It was hard to tell because of her beak, but she almost looked pleased with herself.

"Wait, did the owl warn you I was coming? That's no fair!" Constance protested.

"She also said you had a friend, so hurry up with the grand reveal. Who is it?"

Constance spun around on the counter and eyed Phoebe. "You ruined the surprise as well?!" Phoebe blinked slowly at Constance but said nothing. She started pruning some feathers, as if she hadn't even heard the question. Constance looked back at me. "That thing needs to go." She jerked a thumb in Phoebe's direction.

"On the contrary she's never been more valuable. I told you to quit the jump scares and you didn't listen. Now I have advanced warning of them. Now what's this surprise?"

"No, I don't think I want to tell you now," she said, pouting and crossing her arms. It was really rather amazing how juvenile Constance could act, especially considering that she was at the tail-end of 60.

"Come on Mariah *Scary,* no need to get in a mood."

Once again, my killer pun-work delivered. Constance dropped the upset act and let out a small smile. "Ugh, that was irritatingly good."

"Somewhat less impressive seeing you recycle that for a second time," Hermes said through narrow eyes.

"Shh. No need to ruin it. She wasn't here for the first one."

"What first one?" Constance asked.

"Nothing, never mind. Who's the guest?"

Constance looked down through the kitchen floor and shouted. "Come up, idiot!" Another ghost floated up through the table and made themselves known.

"Bloody hell, it's Kaiser Klaus," I gasped.

"Oh well done, figure that out all by yourself, did you?" he said petulantly.

"Just as lovely in death as life," I said through my teeth. I looked at Constance. "Where did you find him?"

"They always appear near the morgue. He was hovering over his own body criticizing the coroner!" Constance said.

"In my defense she *was* doing a horrible job," the ghost of Kaiser said with a shrug. "Stupid girl dropped a pen inside my open chest!" I grimaced at that mental picture.

Constance floated forward. "Anyway, I told him to stop with the petty little comments and follow me over here. Figured he might have something valuable to say—why I thought that I'd never know."

"Hang on," I said, "I thought you worshipped the ground this moron walks on. You've changed your tune!"

"Yes, I guess I have," Constance realized. "I think since that ring was destroyed my opinion of him has changed drastically."

"Someone destroyed my lucky ring?!" Kaiser asked, horror evident on his face.

"It wasn't lucky, it was cursed," I explained. "And I need to know where you got it from?"

"None of your business, you nosy wretch!" Kaiser spat. Constance leapt forward, grabbed him by the ear and twisted it around. Kaiser started howling. "Stop! Stop, it hurts!"

"Be respectful to my niece, or I'll take you to the sewage treatment plant and shove your face under the waste inlet pipe for an entire day!" she threatened.

"Okay, I'm sorry, I'm sorry!" Kaiser pleaded. "Just let me go!" Constance let go of him and he floated into a standing position again, rubbing the ghostly ear she had nearly ripped off his head. He scowled at her and looked back at me. "I got it from someone woman wearing a hood a few weeks ago. She said it was perfect for someone like me—said I'd bring out the ring's natural qualities, or some rubbish like that."

"Where was this?" I asked.

"Out of town. Down in Vernoy. It's a few hours from here."

"Did she say who she was?"

"Just said she was a fan. I can't remember her name; it was something weird though. It began with an 'M'."

"Morgantha?" Morgantha Hollow was one of the head witches in the Sisters of the Shade. I'd met her once recently when she'd tried to kidnap me.

"That's it," Kaiser said calmly. "Weird hippy name. I was only going to put the ring on for a second, she said she'd made it for me and wanted a photo, but as soon as it was on my finger... I didn't want to take it off."

"A nasty ring for a nasty little man," Constance said. "I can see why she picked him!"

"This about confirms it then, it sounds like Morgantha and her cronies are flooding the town with cursed items—no doubt trying to spread mischief and mayhem."

"Well, it's working!" Constance remarked. "Certainly keeping you busy enough!"

"No kidding," I murmured. I looked at Kaiser. "Listen, I'm trying to solve your murder—for some reason. Any information you might be able to help share?"

"Wait, *you're* the one trying to solve it?" he groaned. "They'll never catch the killer!" Constance sprung forward again and grabbed Kaiser by the ear. "It was a joke, a joke!" he howled.

"Any more jokes and we're going straight to the poop pipe, is that clear?!" she growled.

"Okay, okay!" he wailed. "Just let me go!"

Once Constance released him Kaiser straightened up again and floated away from her a little. "I don't really remember anything, okay —I'm telling the truth. It's like there's this cloud over my memories. Is that normal?"

"Apparently so," I said. "When people die under traumatic circumstances their memory is often cloudy when they wake up as a ghost. I think it's to prevent ghosts from living in permanent trauma. There might be something you can remember though; any little detail might help."

Kaiser thought hard. "Honestly, it's all a blur. The last thing I remember is leaving the stage after announcing the winner. I remember walking back to my dressing room in a bad mood, I was really very disappointed at the selection of entries this year. Not a good baker in this town, I tell you." Kaiser then noticed Constance getting ready to jump him again. "Okay, I take it back, I take it back!"

"What else?" I prompted him.

His brow creased in thought, Kaiser shook his head. "After that it's a blur. I went into my dressing room and—" He paused. "Wait, I think I do remember something. Someone hit me, on the back of my head. When I came to my arms and wrists were bound, and they were talking to me—"

"The killer?" I asked.

He nodded. "Yes, their face is all blurry and… I don't think I knew them."

"You're saying the killer was someone you didn't know?" I asked. "That's… highly unlikely. Murders are almost never random. There's always usually a personal motive involved."

"Well, I guess I'm just a liar then!" Kaiser said. "Honestly, like I said, if you're the one working this thing, we're never going to figure out who killed me. Might as well give the case to a dog for all it matters, I mean really—"

"Right! Sewer treatment plant, here we come!" Constance roared. With one swift movement she flew forward, grabbed Kaiser by the ear and disappeared through the kitchen wall, Kaiser wailing in fear as they passed through the cabinets.

"Things are a lot weirder since you moved here," Hermes said after a long moment.

"My life was perfectly normal before this. It's the town, not me!"

"Hudson. Doorbell," Phoebe announced. Sure enough a moment later the doorbell rang, I went over to the intercom.

"Hudson?" I asked.

"How did you know? I didn't know there was a camera on this thing."

"Less a camera, and more an owl that tells me things three seconds from the future. Hold on I'll buzz you up."

Hudson came up the stairs and into the kitchen. "Morning," he said with a grin that made my knees feel weak. "I guess it's D-day."

"D-day?" I asked.

"Uh yeah, it's been five tides since we met with the sirens. We need to resolve that little problem this morning."

"Right, I kind of glossed over the five tides thing—to be honest I had no idea what it meant."

"It means our deadline is this morning. How did you get on with your side of the plan?" Hudson took a seat at the table and poured himself a cup of coffee.

"My side of the plan? That makes it sound like you've been doing something too."

"I've had my hands full with other things! You don't know half of what goes on in this town. I've spent the last two days clearing out a group of poltergeist settlers! They've been a job and a half, let me tell you!"

"Still no look with your tingly-wingly though, eh?" Hermes said with a smug grin.

"It's called a Tizzie-Whizzie actually, and no—I'm worried. They don't normally disappear unless they're coming back with more—and that would be a real disaster."

"I'm sure it will turn up," Hermes said before leaving the room.

Hudson stared at Hermes for a moment before looking back at me. "Anyway, we have to pay our merfolk friends a visit. Did you track down their missing buddies?" Realizing that I hadn't yet caught Hudson up to date, I went over the siren business with him so far. "So the siren queen is acting crazy because of this cursed necklace..." he surmised.

"Yeah, and I think we're the ones that have to get it off her if we want to make this all kosher."

Hudson grimaced. "Do you know how protective sirens are of their tributes? There's not a chance they'll let us pull that necklace off her, we're going to have to fight."

"I was kind of worried you'd say that actually. I don't think there's much we can do other than go in there with a group and put this problem to rest. If we don't stick to their timeline, they'll just end up snatching someone else from the land. I can get my cousins and Zelda together, that'll give us four witches—with you as well do we stand a fighting chance against these things?"

He thought the question over a few moments before shaking his head. "Honestly, I don't think it's enough. Merfolk magic is powerful, they'll overpower us easily. There's one thing that could give us a real advantage but—" Hudson stopped himself. "Uh, never mind."

"What?" I asked. "What is it?"

"I don't really want to say, because I don't want to go down that route."

"Dude, just tell me!"

Hudson let out a long sigh and closed his eyes. "Sirens are afraid of—"

"Surprise!" Hermes said as he came into the room, walking along behind him was a tiny little hedgehog with bright golden wings. "It was me! I was the one that fixed your problem! I just sat down and talked with the little guy. This is all a big misunderstanding!"

Hudson was frozen with panic, his gaze fixed on the small, winged creature. He whispered to me through his teeth. "Zora don't make any moves. We are in incredible danger."

"Oh stop being so dramatic!" Hermes chuckled. "I told you I talked to Biddyzip—that's his name by the way—he agreed to leave town, he just wanted somewhere to crash."

"Wait, that thing has been sleeping here?" I said in alarm.

"On Constance's bed, yah," Hermes said calmly.

Hudson still looked majorly freaked out, but he seemed a little calmer. "Wait, how did you talk with this thing? They're not communicative."

"To your knowledge at least. I'm a polyglot, Hudson, I speak over six-thousand languages."

"There aren't six-thousand languages in the world!" I pointed out.

"Uh there are when you take random magical languages into account. I actually think I'm the first person to learn the language of these little winged guys. He's pretty funny, very dry sense of humor. He apologizes for beating you up Hudson, says he thought you were challenging him to demonstrate his worthiness. That's kind of a thing back where they come from."

Hudson blinked a few times as he stared at the small creature that had been his torment for the last week. "Uh... no problem? Sorry for attacking you also?"

Hermes communicated the words through a series of chitters and clicks. The little magic hedgehog said something back and Hermes broke out in laughter.

"What did it say?" I asked Hermes.

"Oh, I can't tell you, this thing has got a wicked sense of humor. Anyway, I guess you owe me one Hudson. I'll decide what the favor is later."

"I think I'd rather get beat up again..." Hudson groaned.

I looked at him, recalling what we'd been talking about before Hermes came in here with his grand reveal. "Hey, I'm still waiting.

What's this secret weapon you refuse to use? You were about to tell me what sirens are afraid of."

Hudson smiled awkwardly and scratched the back of his head. "It's uh... werewolves," he said with another sigh. "They're afraid of werewolves."

"Ah," I said, realizing why he'd been so reluctant to deliver that information. It looked like Blake had just joined our mission.

CHAPTER 20

I spent the rest of the morning getting everyone together, and then we convened at Hudson's secret underground dock in the burned-out arcade. It was me, Celeste, Sabrina, Zelda, the two runaway sirens, Blake, and Hudson of course.

"McNally's!" Zelda said fondly as we walked inside the old arcade. "I've not been in here since I was a kid."

It was the exact same thing she'd said last time we'd been here, but she couldn't remember the previous visit because Hudson had blanked our memories. For some reasons MAGE's mind-blanking technology wasn't as effective on me, as I distinctly recalled this location from last time.

We walked into the high-tech underground dock and Blake just shook his head and tutted. "Just what exactly is that organization of yours doing with all this hidden gear? Plotting to take over?"

Blake was highly distrustful of Hudson and MAGE, and Hudson held the same level of contempt towards Blake. I kind of hoped they'd put their differences aside while we dealt with the sirens, but I should have known better.

Hudson rolled his eyes and squared up to Blake. They were both equally massive, standing only inches from one another as they got ready to throw down again. "Just for the record I didn't want you here, you're welcome to leave at any time."

Blake scoffed. "And leave you alone to let Zora get mangled? I don't think so. There's a reason these creatures are afraid of my kind—once this mission is over you'll have learned a thing or two about respect."

"We'll see about that," Hudson said through his teeth.

Things didn't ease up at all on the boat ride over to the underground lair. I had Hudson and Blake sit at opposite ends of the boat from one another, but the energy between them was tangible. It felt like sitting in between two opposing magnets.

The 'plan' was pretty simple, once we arrived at the lair the two sirens would change back into their merfolk form and rejoin the tribe. Once Edra and her folks released Gordo, we'd make a move for the necklace. The finer details mostly consisted of 'throw everything we've got at them and hope it sticks'—it would remain to be seen whether that would be enough.

When we arrived at the tunnel to the underground stream the sirens rose up out of the water again. "Did you bring another tribute?"

"Got it right here," Hudson said, lifting up another black backpack containing rare sea treasures. The sirens took it from him warily and inspected the gift. Seemingly satisfied, they closed the backpack and nodded.

"Why are there so many of you this time?" one of the guards questioned, their black eyes glancing over at Blake in particular.

"These are all associates from the organization I work for," Hudson said. "After we make our peace, we hope to perhaps learn a few things about your kind for our records. All those here on this boat are scholars—nothing more. We recognize that the dawn of the merfolk is just beginning, it's a privilege to witness the ascent of a truly superior race."

The guards discussed Hudson's message alone in private for a minute. "Very well," one said as it came back to the front. "You are wise to acknowledge the superiority of the merfolk. Come this way, we will take you to Queen Edra to complete the deal."

And so we made the descent again, our boat following the twisting waterways that ran underneath the town of Compass Cove, heading deeper into the cold caves until we reached the rocky shore to disembark. The sirens escorted us to the hidden treasure room, where Queen Edra and her consort lay in wait.

"Ah," she said, rising from a reclined position to acknowledge us as we stopped before her. "You finally return, and you bring back those we have lost. Excellent."

My eyes were fixed on the siren queen, but in all truth, I was staring at the cursed necklace around her neck. There was no mistaking it this time, the unusual piece looked very similar to the ring that had been on Kaiser's finger. Edra and her entourage were about fifteen feet away from us—close, but not yet close enough.

"Come forward, return to your true form," she said to her runaway sirens. They both walked forward to the pool of azure water and morphed back into merfolk. Edra seemed largely satisfied at finally getting what she wanted, but her smile faded quickly. "Release the other human," she said to one of her guards. "Return him."

A moment later Gordo came back into the room. He still looked well, even though he had been their prisoner. He reunited with our group, and I breathed a sigh of relief to finally have him back. Things were going well.

"My guards inform me you wish to conduct some sort of scholarly questioning out of intrigue?" Edra recapped hazily. "I'm afraid I will have to shut down that idea—we have much work to do, we must set about executing the traitors that have brought so much shame to our tribe. You and your friends are now—"

"Hold on a second," I interrupted. "You said nothing about executing them!"

"Why, of course not," Edra said coyly. "If I'd made my true intentions clear you would never have brought them to me. You will leave now, pray your foolishness does not delay me a second longer—if you're still here when the executions have begun, we will take you all to the depths and you may join our numbers."

I gave Hudson an unsure look, one that he mirrored back at me. I knew we would have to fight at some point, but I hadn't anticipated Edra to push us onto the backfoot like this. "Now listen here—" Hudson began, but before he could finish talking Blake stepped forward and pushed in front.

"I think we're done talking here," he snarled. "So let's get straight to business, shall we?"

Without another word the change came over Blake suddenly. One moment he was standing there as a man, and the next moment there was an explosion of shredded clothes and thick fur. In the blink of an eye a huge wolf was in front of us, so large it was almost the size of a horse. It was the first time I had seen him shift into a wolf, and I couldn't quite believe what I was seeing.

As soon as the change happened the merfolk in the chamber started freaking out. They all readied their weapons and simultaneously moved back out of fear. Edra however just threw her head back and roared with laughter. "Now we see the true colors! They came here to intimidate us, to scare us! Well, I am not scared of a foul beast such as this! If you want war, you've got one, get them!"

In her madness the siren queen might not have been scared of Blake in his wolf form, but the rest of her subjects certainly were. For a brief second none of them did anything, so Blake just let out a huge snarl and leapt forward to tackle the queen to the ground.

As he did so the siren queen reacted in a flash, spinning her trident and sending a charge of molten red magic in Blake's direction. The beam of light hit him and sent him flying into a rock wall with a sickening crunch. As he hit the ground a lattice of blue light wrapped around his body. Edra's necklace was glowing with the blue light too —its magic had Blake trapped.

With Blake down the rest of the merfolk found their courage and the real chaos erupted. Beams of light and flashes of color erupted through the underground cave as magic spells went off in all directions. The siren creatures rushed forward and surrounded us, their tridents blasting bolts of powerful magic.

To say that I wasn't prepared for a brawl with a mad merfolk tribe was an understatement—up until now I'd only learned the very basics of magic, and I knew nothing about magical combat—especially with advanced creatures like this.

With that said I did have a few tricks up my sleeve, and I used all of them. Zelda had taught me a quick shielding spell, and as soon as Blake had hit the wall, the first thing I did was throw a magical shield up around myself. Looking around I saw my cousins had done the same. In terms of offense, I only had two moves, small blasts of fire and the ability to hurl invisible baseball-sized projectiles.

As multiple magical attacks came my way, I employed all of the above, while trying to dodge and dive out of harm's way.

"Get off, get off me!" Zelda shouted as two of the sirens grabbed hold of her and started dragging her out of the main chamber. I was preoccupied with my own siren, who was blasting a flurry of red beams at me. The red rails of light shattered harmlessly off my shield, but I could feel the protective spell taking a battering, I didn't have much longer.

"Will you just… go away already!" I roared in frustration. With that wave of emotion, a huge wall of pressure exploded from the tip of my wand and sent a group of the merfolk flying through the air. With no time to act surprised I ran after the two sirens trying to take my sister away. "Hey!" I yelled, they turned around as I got their attention. "Look down!"

The two-merfolk looked at their feet and there they saw the convincing illusion of two wolves snapping at their heels. I'd used prestidigitation to put the image in their minds. They shrieked, dropped Zelda and ran off screaming.

"Thanks, I owe you one!" she huffed as I helped her up. Turning around I saw Celeste and Sabrina back-to-back, trying to protect Gordo as a circle of sirens closed in on them. Blake was still unconscious on the ground, and Hudson was locked in a battle with the siren queen herself, somehow holding his own against the strong and insane merwoman.

"Help!" Sabrina shouted over to us. "I'm pretty much out of magic!"

"Me too!" Celeste said, sending a few feeble blasts at their approaching attackers.

Zelda and I ran forward to help them, but admittedly I was feeling low on magic myself, I didn't know much more I could give—and I knew that Zelda would be feeling the same.

With a furious roar I slashed my wand through the air and sent another wall of force blasting across the cavern. The ferocious wind picked up the sirens circling on my cousins and sent their attackers hurtling. Somehow it didn't move Sabrina, Celeste, or Gordo—it was like my magic had automatically made them exempt from the attack.

"That all you got?!" Edra roared from our right. Looking over I saw her strike Hudson hard with a blow, one that sent him flying into a wall. When he hit the ground another grid of blue magical light came over him, pinning him to the ground, much the same as Blake. I shoved my wand into my back pocket to run over to him, but the demonic siren queen turned her glowing black eyes on us and stalked forward, laughing darkly as she closed the distance. We'd fought off her minions, but Edra barely seemed phased by the attack.

"Change of plan. You're all coming to the depths!" She lifted her trident and roared something in their ancient merfolk magic. *"Draksa Yahti!"*

WITH THE WORDS a dozen black cords shot out the end of her trident and started wrapping around us all, binding us from head to toe until we dropped to the ground, encased like mummies, unable to escape. I realized the black cords were in fact seaweed—leathery, tough, cold, and sharp.

I had fallen awkwardly and landed on a rock, the wand in my back pocket digging into my back. Edra walked forward and surveyed her new prisoners, her eyes shining with malice.

"Our numbers will grow greatly today. The ocean has brought us a real blessing. Concede defeat witches and I will go easy on you—I can feel that your magic is gone."

"Go to hell!" Celeste hissed. It was clear the four of us were struggling and no longer had any magic left to fight—the encounter had drained us all of our magical and physical strength. We lay there struggling against the binds, knowing that we'd lost the fight.

"You will learn to respect me once the transformation happens," Edra said assuredly. "In time you will all learn. We will begin the transformation at once, starting with that one—" Edra pointed at Celeste. "Guards, stop cowering and get over here! We go to the depths at once!"

I lay there looking at the cave ceiling, wishing I could summon one last bolt of strength to try and fight back, but without magic I couldn't do anything.

If I just had a small top up... That's when an idea came to me. At once I started squirming on the ground, grimacing as the wand digging into my back bent over the rock underneath me.

"Zora, stay still!" Zelda hissed. "What are you doing, we're not getting out of this now!"

"I'm putting all my trust in the promises of a salesman. So here goes nothing!"

My wand broke with a crisp 'crack!', emitting a small explosion of warm light that quickly fizzled out. For a second nothing happened, but then—

He popped into thin air like an angel sent from sales heaven. Clarence Hogman stood before me with a new wand held out in the air. "Zora Wick, keen to test out that premium insurance I see! Well let's hand over your replacement wand and—" Clarence paused upon seeing me and my cousins bound in seaweed, surrounded by a tribe of mad merfolk in an underground cave. "...Not going to lie, I wasn't expecting this."

"Another one?!" Edra roared on her way back to her pearl plinth. "Seize him, guards!"

"Quick!" I shouted to Clarence. "You said I get a replacement wand and a free magical top up, right?"

"Right!" he stammered. "Coming up!" Clarence squealed as a dozen of the siren guards rushed towards him. With a snap of his fingers, I felt my magic powers replenish, just as Clarence got tackled to the ground. My replacement wand flew through the air in slow motion, I blasted the bindings off my body, jumped to my feet, caught the wand, and pointed the tip at the siren queen halfway across the chamber.

With my eyes focused on the cursed necklace around Edra's throat I put every ounce of my magical energy forward and bellowed a singular word. "Necklace!"

The necklace ripped off Edra's throat and flew right at me, I held my hand out to catch it, but the blasted thing slipped through my fingers, smashed into my face and dropped me to the ground.

"Give it back! Give it back!" Edra screamed. Pushing myself up onto my elbows I saw her rushing right at me. Just then two figures closed in on her from the left and right, the giant bounding form of Blake as a wolf on the left, and the charging figure of Hudson on the right, his eyes burning bright with some sort of ferocious magic.

They took her down at the same time and she came crashing to the ground. Hudson looked over at me and shouted. "Destroy it!" Without needing another prompt, I grabbed the necklace off my face and swung it down hard against the ground, the black pearls shattering over the rock. As they splintered into tiny shards the dark magic in the necklace washed out harmlessly over the ground—the curse was finished.

All of a sudden the siren queen pushed herself up from the ground and looked around in confusion, unsure why a werewolf and a magically enhanced human had her pinned to the ground. "What on earth is going on here?" she asked.

I breathed a sigh of relief and dropped my head to the ground.

It was over.

CHAPTER 21

After the hazardous encounter I anticipated more problems would follow. We may have freed the siren queen from her curse, but our little intervention had caused quite the scene. Fortunately, as soon as the necklace was destroyed a change came over the siren queen and her people. Her guards actually helped us out of the bounds, lifted us to our feet and for the first time the strange aquatic people didn't feel overtly hostile.

"I am in your debt," Edra said after everyone had collected themselves. "The whole time I had that thing on I knew what it was doing to me, but I couldn't stop it. It's like I was sitting in the backseat of my own mind. Truly, we are forever grateful to you and your friends—Zora Wick."

"Just trying to right the wrongs of the witches that gave you the necklace in the first place," I said. Edra nodded as though she understood.

"Regardless, name your terms and we will agree to them. Our kind may not have always got along well, but today I feel the tide change—this is a new beginning for our people. What do you need?"

Everyone looked at me as I considered the question. "...Honestly, I just want things to be okay between us. I hear relationships between the witches and sirens of Compass Cove have always been a little frigid—hopefully we can make steps to changing that relationship." I then quickly added. "Oh, and please don't take any humans to the depths."

Edra looked at me knowingly. "Ask, and you shall receive. We are allies now, and I hope this is the beginning of a fortuitous relationship. As thanks we will make the rare honor of giving each person in your party a parting piece of tribute. May these items bless you—may the tide always roll in your favor—and may the water wash away the strain of our mutual pasts!"

Not long after that our group assembled and went back to Hudson's. We navigated the waterways and soon we were back at the entrance to the caves, where the sirens warmly bid us goodbye. As we sped over the water a strange excitement swept through the group. We went over the crazy events of the last hour, all of us holding a unique piece of tribute awarded by the sirens. My gift was a pastel pink conch shell with a crown of orange tips spiraling over its surface —truly it was beautiful.

"I can't believe we actually got out of there alive!" Celeste said in amazement. "I thought for sure we were all goners!"

"I had my doubts too," Sabrina confessed. "Quick thinking by deliberately breaking your wand, Zora, I've never seen a wand insurance salesman look so shocked before!"

In part it was Clarence that had saved the day, without his relentless badgering I'd never have caved and bought his stupid policy in the first place. He'd stuck around for a little bit before our boat set sail from the underground shoal beach. Clarence had disappeared by crawling into a hole in the rocks.

"What's with weird entrances and exits, by the way? Every time I see that guy he's crawling into some absurdly small gap," I noted.

"They have access to Couch Space," Zelda explained. "It's this weird little pocket dimension where lost things usually end up. They've had run of it for a while now—I've never actually seen one pop into thin air before, you must have sprung for a premium package!"

Once we got back to Hudson's secret dock, we all climbed out of the boat and made our way to the parking lot outside. I was halfway there when I realized that Blake and Hudson hadn't followed us. I turned back down the hallway and went to open the door back to the dock room when I heard them talking in quiet voices. Peeping through the door I saw them both standing about ten feet away from one another.

"You did well back there," Blake said to Hudson. "Thanks for looking out for Zora."

"Likewise. I couldn't have kept that thing held down on my own," Hudson replied.

"Just for the record, I still don't trust you—but I guess you deserve credit—those creatures are no joke, and you held your ground."

Hudson smiled ever so slightly. "I don't trust you either—but I think I might hate you five percent less."

"Generous, I only hate you one percent less," Blake said.

"Alright, get out of my dock, and Blake?" Blake had started walking away but turned back to look at Hudson. Hudson snapped his fingers and blue motes of light shimmered in the air. "You can't remember any of this."

With Blake coming my way I quickly ran outside into the lot, where Blake and Hudson met us a moment later. The girls waited in the van while I talked to them. "Time for me to go," Blake said to me. "You did well back there."

"Thanks, you too." I looked at Blake, who was now back in his human form, his police uniform intact. "I saw your clothes explode and then you were a wolf—did you bring a spare set or something?"

Blake grinned, he curled his right forearm and the arm momentarily shifted into a huge wolf paw, the arm of his uniform ripped up to the shoulder. Blake then eased off, and the wolf part shifted back into a human arm. As it did so the shredded uniform came back together, like I was watching it in reverse.

"The shift uses temporal magic," he explained. "It's… hard to explain."

"I think I get it?" I said, though I wasn't completely sure. "Let's meet up tomorrow—we still have a killer to catch."

He nodded and then with a monumental leap he disappeared into the sky, heading back in the direction of town. I turned and looked at Hudson.

"Another zany day for Zora Wick," he said with a warm smile.

"What can I say? I like to keep things interesting. Thanks for all the help, we couldn't have done this without you."

"You're the one that saved our bacon at the end of the day," he said. "By the way it's a pretty huge deal to receive tributes from a siren tribe. I think we've made some serious allies today—you're going to be a gift to this town and its magic population Zora, I can tell."

"Stop, you're making me blush," I joked. "Thanks for burying the hatchet with Blake, by the way. I overheard you both talking."

Hudson shrugged. "He won't remember anyway, had to blank his memory."

"Still, it means a lot to me that you're both making steps forward. I know it's not easy for either of you. I won't forget this."

He smiled at me in a knowing way then and raised his fingers. I saw the blue motes of light dancing on the air before he did the snap. "You sure about that?"

* * *

THE NEXT DAY I met Blake down at the police station, I hadn't actually gone there to meet him explicitly, but figured I'd be the one to show up at this workplace for once.

"Zora," he said with surprise as I walked into the station. "I was just about to come over to the bakery to check up on you."

"Guess I beat you to it. I actually came here because I wanted to speak with Tamara Banana. Is she around?"

"The woman from CSI? The coroner? No, she doesn't work in this building. Her office is down at the morgue. I can take you there if you like?"

"Lead the way wolf boy," I said.

We both left the station and headed towards the morgue in Blake's cruiser. "What did you want to talk to her about anyway?" Blake asked as he drove through town.

"My Aunt Constance showed up the other day with Kaiser Klaus' ghost. I think I might have a small lead."

"You didn't mention anything about seeing his ghost!" Blake looked over at me.

"Yeah, sorry, I've had a lot on my plate at the moment. The siren thing kind of got out of control really fast—now it's sorted I can focus my efforts in one direction again."

"What's the lead then?" Blake asked. "Did he see the killer?"

"He can't remember most of it. Most ghosts have amnesia if they die under traumatic circumstances, he claimed to remember getting hit on the head though. I figured Tamara might be able to shed a little more light on whether or not that actually happened."

"I'm confused." Blake's hands moved over the wheel as he made a left turn. "How is this going to catch a killer?"

I shrugged. "I don't have all the answers yet, I'm just following the one lead we *do* have. Wait, do we have to pass the voodoo bakery to get to the morgue? Pull over, we're getting sandwiches!"

"Seriously?" Blake groaned.

"Just pull over already!"

With an audible huff Blake pulled over and we walked in the direction of Mistress Bridgette's voodoo bakery. As ever there was a line stretching around the block, I went to join the back of it when Blake grabbed my hand and pulled me towards the shop.

"What are you doing?" I asked.

"You think I'm spending an hour in this line? We're police, let's just say we're here to ask questions."

"Dude, that's not cool!" I said to him. But it did mean not waiting for a delicious sandwich. I then realized we were still holding hands as we reached the shop. I pulled my hand out of Blake's and there was an awkward moment between us.

"Police business!" Blake shouted and walked into the shop. "Coming through!"

We walked inside the busy shop and saw Mistress Bridgette behind the counter with her assistants. "Now there's a pair of faces I wasn't expecting to see today. How can I help you both?"

"We uh…" I said. Blake had really dropped me in it now. I didn't have any questions for Mistress Bridgette after our talk the other day, but he'd just marched in here shouting about police business. "Can we talk for a quick minute?"

"Of course, let's go up to the office." We followed her upstairs and sat down at the desk. "So, what did you want to know?" she asked.

"Go on Blake," I said, nudging him in the arm.

"What? I thought we just came in here for sandwiches!" he said obliviously.

I dropped my head into my hand. "You are literally the worst."

Mistress Bridgette however broke out in laughter. "Ah, I get it. Didn't want to wait in line? I understand one hundred percent. If you have no questions we can head back downstairs, and I'll ring up your orders."

I then remembered something from the day of Kaiser's death. It was a lightbulb moment, when Mistress Bridgette had been on stage with him. She had snapped her fingers and sprinkled something on the stage right before storming off.

"Actually, I do have a question. When you left the stage, you sprinkled something in front of Kaiser Klaus. What was that?"

"Ah that be me Zangbeto dust, it's a special concoction—I was trying to air out whatever bad spirit was hanging around that man."

"But you said, 'May you get what's coming to you', it sounded like you were cursing him," I noted.

Mistress Bridgette shook her head. "No, I was talking to whatever spirit was afflicting him. I figured something wicked was hanging around him because he was such a horror." She looked at me for a moment and added, "I already told you my voodoo is a white magic—I am not a dark witch Miss Wick, even if you think me to be one."

"I don't—" I began, but she cut me off.

"Do not worry about explaining your perceptions, I hold no judgements against you. You are a witch with intuition, and you know that

I am keeping something from you. That's what makes you so suspicious of me."

"Well, yes," I said, a little surprised she had laid it all out so clearly. "So why not just come out and tell me what you're hiding?"

"I'm afraid it's not that simple... and some things are better left unsaid. All I will say is this—watch your back, I see danger in your future." The phrase had all the makings of a threat, but the way she said them made it feel like it came from a place of concern. I left the office feeling more confused than ever—could I trust this woman or not?

After grabbing our sandwiches (I devoured my immediately) we headed to the morgue to speak with Tamara. We found her sitting on reception, playing a videogame on the computer.

"What?" she asked as we walked in. "It's not always busy around here!"

"Well, I've got some work for you. It's about Kaiser Klaus, did you find any blunt force trauma on the head when you did the autopsy?"

"No, something like that would be easy to spot as well. The guy was balding!"

"Is there a chance you could have missed something?" Blake asked. "Do you think you could check again."

Tamara made an unsure face. "I don't know, I *am* pretty busy this morning..." She looked up from her screen and winked. "Just kidding. Let's go and check a dead guy's skull, eh? Let me get you some guest passes first, can let any old rabble wander into the back."

We followed Tamara into the back of the morgue, a large cold room with a wall of 12 metal doors for the body refrigeration unit. Tamara opened a door in the middle row on the far right and pulled out the slab. There upon it was a black body bag. She unzipped it and there was the cold grey body of Kaiser Klaus.

"Yeah, see?" she said as she crouched down and pointed at the shiny bald dome. She put on gloves and moved her fingers over the surface. "If he'd been hit in the head there would be visible bruising to indicate—huh." Tamara paused as her fingers found something on the back of Kaiser's skull.

"What is it?" I asked.

"There *is* something here. I can't believe I missed it. A small, depressed fracture at the rear of the skull. It's very slight, he was hit with a small point very quickly. There is a bruise, but it's so small, I thought it was a liver spot!"

"That confirms it then," I said to Blake. "The killer came into the room and hit Kaiser on the back of the head. When he was down, they tied him up and stabbed him."

"If he was down then why not just stab him?" Blake asked.

I shrugged. "Maybe they had something to say."

"I'm going to go over the body in case I missed anything else," Tamara said. "I can't believe I missed this, seriously embarrassing!"

"Don't worry about it, you *did* see the mark—you mistook it for something else." I looked at Blake. "We need to go back to the crime scene and see if we can source the item that caused the fracture. There's a chance the killer might have left their prints on it!"

"Oh, I can drive with the sirens on!" Blake said excitedly.

"If we get a moment, we could even grab another sandwich from Bridgette's!" Blake's deadpan stare told me the answer to that one. "No? Worth a shot though, right? Blake? Wait for me! Blake!"

CHAPTER 22

We climbed through the police tape zig-zagged across the door and stepped into the crime scene once again. The room was quiet and empty, a patch of carpet cut away where Kaiser's body had bled onto the floor. We both began looking for the small object that could have caused the blunt-impact trauma.

"What are we looking for?" Blake asked. "It could be anything!" He picked up a hairbrush from a vanity table and put it down again.

"I don't know. There's a good chance it's not even here, we just need to try and think like the killer." Looking around the room I couldn't see anything that would suitably match the profile of Tamara's description. Kaiser had been hit in the back of head by something small, and from the impact Tamara said the hit was quick. "Did the killer throw something at him?"

"You know what I think? We need to try and retrace the killer's steps. How did they get to this room?" Blake walked out of the dressing room and looked in the direction of the double doors leading into the empty convention hall. "Through there?"

"No," I said with a shake of my head. "There were guards stationed there, they weren't letting anyone through."

"How did you get through then?" Blake asked.

"The old 'trick them into thinking their butts are on fire' trick. I'm quite sophisticated with this magic stuff you know?"

Blake laughed. "Yeah, I can see that. So let's rule out those double doors, the killer got to the dressing room another way, but how?"

We both walked through the back corridors of the hall, mapping the potential routes and exits from the building. On this side of the building there was only one actual exit to the exterior—a set of fire doors at the very back.

"The killer had to come through here then," Blake mused as we opened the doors and walked outside. It was a sunny day, the sky was blue and the sun was shining brightly. At the rear of the building there was a small lot and the back entrances to other surrounding buildings. Several large metal dumpsters were lined up outside the rear fire exit. I walked over to the nearest one and threw it open.

"Please don't tell me you're going to go dumpster diving in that thing," he said.

"That sounds more like a job for my keeper, don't you think?"

Blake laughed. "Think again. We have no reason to be crawling through trash."

"The killer came in and out through this door, there's a very good chance they disposed of their attack weapon in this dumpster. Now get in there wolf boy."

"It's my job to keep you safe from physical threats." Blake peered over the edge of the dumpster and looked at me. "Visual assessment complete. Looks safe. Go right ahead."

"Eh, it was worth a shot. Help me get in then." Blake held his hand out, I put my foot into it and he lifted me up with ease. I let out a little yelp at the unexpected speed and went flying over the metal lip and into the dumpster. "Not funny!" I shouted to him.

"Oh, it's pretty funny from where I'm standing," he cackled. For good measure I picked up a moldy banana skin and threw it at him. "Gross! Not funny!"

"It's pretty funny from where I'm sitting," I countered.

"Touché," Blake said grumpily.

After a few minutes of dumpster diving I gave up and Blake helped me to climb out again. As I hopped onto the ground and stood up I saw Constance floating over towards me, with Kaiser Klaus in tow. "Oh great," I muttered.

"What?" Blake asked, looking around obliviously. He didn't have the ability to see ghosts like me.

"It's my Aunt Constance and the ghost of our dearly departed bread judge."

"What are you doing here?!" Constance said as she floated on over.

"Doing the whole murder solving business, remember?" I looked at Kaiser's ghost, anticipating the catty comment from him.

"I'm sure you'll crack it in no time, keep at it!" he said through a forced smile. I narrowed my eyes at him suspiciously.

"Why is he acting so weird?"

"Oh a few hours under the waste inlet pipe at the sewer treatment plant will do that," Constance said cheerily.

"Can ghosts even smell?"

"New ghosts can," Constance said with an evil grin. "Takes a while to completely lose taste and smell."

"Oh my..." I looked at Kaiser as I contemplated the true horror of Constance's unusual punishment. "That's why you're being so nice then."

If Kaiser wasn't a ghost his face would definitely be deathly pale. "Constance has been great! She's really showing me the ropes of being a ghost. Can't fault her!" Despite the glowing review Kaiser reminded me of those videos where hostages had nothing but praise for their captors.

"Blink twice if she's holding a gun to your head," I joked and looked back at Constance. "What are you doing here?"

"I find it helps new ghosts to adjust to the afterlife if we revisit the scene of their death every now and then. You'd be surprised how whiny people are after dying. *'Oh Constance, it was before my time! Oh Constance, I had so much left to give! I don't want to be dead!'*"

"I told you those things in strict confidence!" Kaiser said, looking embarrassed.

"Cry on your own time!" she snapped, before looking at me again.

"Anyway, I keep dragging them back to their death place until they get bored of it. I basically force them to move on, I've not got any time for this complaining. You know what I did when I woke up as a ghost? I got on with things!"

"Not everyone can adjust to change like you," I pointed out. "And dying is a pretty big change. A little sympathy might go along way!"

"There's no sympathy for the dead, Zora, ever heard that expression before?"

"I don't know why I try and reason with you." I turned my attention. "Some good news—we confirmed what you told us. The coroner found a small impact trauma at the back of your head. Said you were hit very quickly with something small."

"I told you!" Kaiser said. "I wasn't lying!"

"We came here to try and find the attack weapon, but we're not having any luck so far." Looking over at Blake, I saw him studying the brick wall next to the fire doors. He had crouched down and picked something off the floor, holding it between his fingers. "What are you doing dude?"

"I thought I'd look around while you had your ghost conversation. It's a bit difficult to keep up when I can't hear the other side, so I thought I'd make myself useful."

"By picking up bits of dirt off the ground?"

"Not dirt, it's brick. Look." I came over and got a closer look at the brick chipping. "It came from this wall here." Blake stood up and pointed at the wall. There were several small marks in the wall, it looked like someone had gone haywire with a chisel.

"Oh, that was from that weird girl," Constance said casually. I turned around and looked at her.

"Weird girl?" I asked. "What weird girl?"

"I saw her out here on the day of the bread fair. She had this little metal thing on the end of a cord, and she was spinning it around and slinging it against the wall! Did some damage as well from the looks of thing, the little vandal!"

"Constance that is extremely unusual. Why didn't you say anything?"

"Zora you see people do unusual things all the time when you're a ghost. The living do very weird things when no one else is around."

"What's she saying?" Blake asked. From his perspective I was talking to thin air. I recapped Constance's story. "Wait, could that be the attack weapon?"

"How old was this girl? Did you see where she went after this?"

"Maybe the same age as you? She went inside through those doors there." I looked at the doors and then at Blake.

"I think this woman might be our killer! Constance says she went inside!"

"What did she look like?" Blake asked. "Do you think it was Gwen Garner? Or Bridgette?"

"She looked very normal," Constance said to me. "Brown hair... very average face. White. Is that one of your suspects?!" she asked with excitement.

"No," I said. Gwen Garner was blonde, and Bridgette wasn't white. That meant the killer was someone else altogether, someone that hadn't been a suspect.

"What was she slinging against the wall?" Blake asked. He was trying to talk to Constance directly, but as he couldn't see her, he was staring ever so slightly in the wrong direction.

"Oh, I don't know, one of them small metal loops. People use them to tie down loads sometimes. They've got a funny name, a Caribbean or something like that?"

I froze as she said the word. "Wait a second, you mean a carabiner!"

"Yes!" she said. "That's the one, carabiner!"

"Slingies..." I muttered to myself.

"What?" Blake asked.

"It was a carabiner!" I said to Blake. "This woman had a carabiner on the end of a cord! She must have used it to hit Klaus on the back of the head!"

Blake's eyes suddenly widened in realization. "You know who uses a lot of carabiners? Climbers!" His excitement faded. "But... we already ruled out the dude at the climbing center."

"We ruled *him* out, but the killer was there the whole time, right under our noses. The clues all point to her, and she even had motive! We have to get there, now!"

"Well let's go then!" he said, and we started running in the direction of Blake's cruiser.

* * *

As TEMPTING as it was to run into the climbing center, we walked in calmly so not to scare away the suspect. We approached the main desk and found Gareth Taylor, our first suspect in this case.

"Ah, hello again!" he said cheerily. "Wasn't expecting to see you here again so soon. Has there been a development in the case?"

"Yes, we need to talk to your girlfriend, Maddie. Is she around?"

A look of confusion came over Gareth's face. "Maddie, yeah, she's just back there running some lessons, why do you need to—hey, wait!"

Blake and I marched past the desk and walked quickly towards the climbing walls. Sure enough Maddie was right at the back, standing on the ground and holding climbing ropes as a young boy scaled the wall high above. She must have seen us in her peripheral vision, when we were about twenty feet away she looked over and then started running.

"She's fleeing!" I said, beginning to give chase. As Maddie dropped the ropes the young boy climbing at the top of the wall slipped off his holds and started falling. "Blake, catch him!" I yelled.

"On it!"

Though Blake didn't like using his super speed in front of the public he wasted no time making sure that he caught the boy. I was sprinting at full speed now, my eyes fixed on Maddie as she disappeared through a door in the back.

"Wait up!" Blake shouted as he set the boy down and sprinted after me. As I went through the door, I found myself in a corridor filled with open boxes of climbing supplies. I saw Maddie disappear around another corner as she continued to flee.

"That's far enough!" I shouted to her. "Give yourself up!"

"No!" she shouted back. "That man ruined everything for me!"

As I came around the corner, I saw Maddie waiting there for me, a small pocketknife in her hands. "I'm sorry, but I'm not going to jail for this! I'm not a bad person!"

Before I could react, she lunged forward and buried the knife in my stomach. I dropped to the floor and gasped for breath. Maddie's knife clattered to the ground, she turned around and made her way for the rear doors.

"No!" Blake screamed. He blurred past me as a supersonic flash and pinned Maddie against the wall. He cuffed her to a pipe on the wall and in a second he was back, crouched over me, holding me in his arms. "Zora! No!" he said, panic and desperation evident on his face.

"I'm fine," I wheezed. Looking down at my torso I expected to see a torrent of bright red blood, but to my surprise there was nothing. "What in the..." I gasped.

"That's impossible!" Blake said. "How are you—" he then picked up the knife Maddie had dropped on the ground. It was bent around like a horseshoe, like someone had stuck it into a vice and pulled the handle down. Blake was as confused as me. "How in the world? Do you have a stab vest on?"

"Nothing!" I stammered, standing to my feet and patting my stomach, unable to believe I was alive and uninjured. It didn't make any sense, but as I patted myself over, I felt something in my pocket—something I didn't know was there. "What the..." I mumbled as I pulled out a small voodoo fetish made out of white knotted string. The little doll was warm to the touch, and I felt the prickle of magic crackling from its surface. I looked up at Blake. "Mistress Bridgette, she must have slipped this in my pocket."

"I guess she was telling the truth after all about being a good witch. The magic from that thing must have kept you safe!"

"Come on, let's talk to our purp." Blake helped me up to my feet and we walked over to Maddie, was who still cuffed to the pipe.

"Just for the record we'll be throwing an attempted murder charge on top of everything else you've done," Blake growled.

Maddie looked at me, fraught with stress. "How did you figure it out?!" she said in defeat.

"The clues pointed to you all along," I said. "We just weren't looking closely enough. Cinnamon paste left on the knife handle... you told us you eat a Cinnabon every morning! Cat fur... your boyfriend Gareth told us you were a 'fur momma'. And the knots on the ropes around Kaiser's hands and feet—well they came from someone who knew what they were doing. We missed a few things, but once we found them it all added up. Sharp impact trauma to the back of the head, pretty easy for a girl that has won trophies for knocking down tin cans with a climbing clip! You walked in there, whipped him with a carabiner to knock him down and then tied him up. Why? Why not just stab him there and then?"

"I wanted to give him a piece of my mind! He destroyed Gareth's life! He destroyed my life! Gareth and I were going to get married! So I knocked him down, tied him up, told him what he needed to hear! He was so scared he had nothing to say, for once in his life! I killed him, and I'd kill him again!"

"Save it for the judge," Blake said. "Ma'am, I am placing you under arrest. Anything you say can and will be used against you a court of law. You have the right to an attorney; you have the right..."

As Blake continued he led Maddie back to the cruiser, I looked at the little white doll in my hands. It seemed I'd been looking at the wrong person this entire time—I owed Bridgette an apology, her magic had saved my life after all.

Maybe while I was there I could get a couple more sandwiches too?

CHAPTER 23

ONE WEEK LATER

"What a day!" Daphne said as she turned the sign on the door to closed. "I think that has to be a record breaker!"

"Judging by the amount of money on the register I would say you're right," I said, wiping the back of my hand over my sweaty forehead. I plonked myself down into a chair and had a big drink of water. Business had been fantastic over the last week, and for the first time since taking over the bakery I was going to close this month with profit.

Daphne sat down across from me and started scrolling through her phone. "We should get out in that mobile bakery van at some point. I bet we could get even more business in that thing!"

"The van worked great last time we tried it. Ideally, we'd have two people in the van and at least one person here at the shop..." I started crunching numbers in my head, wondering if I could afford to do that yet.

"You'd have to advertise for a job vacancy again and do more interviews!" Daphne pointed out.

"Ugh... I hadn't actually considered that. Maybe I'll hold off on expanding the empire for now." *Sorry Oprah, you're going to have to wait for that interview.*

"Any plans for tonight?" Daphne asked.

"Yes, I'm putting my pajamas on and falling asleep in front of a bad rom com. You?"

"I have a date actually—some guy I met through a dating app."

"Ooh," I said. "Got a picture?"

"As a matter of fact, I do..." Daphne turned her phone around to show me a picture of a pale guy with dark hair.

"Woah, he's a smoke show! ...Maybe I should get on a dating app."

Daphne smirked. "Why? You've already got two hot guys clamoring after you."

"Blake and Hudson? I think of them more like co-workers—it's a weird arrangement. Besides, they've probably got their own thing going on." Daphne gave me a weird look. "What?!"

"Dude I've seen how they both look at you. They have nothing else going on, trust me. Anyway, they're not your co-workers, they're your *guardians.* Didn't you ever see the bodyguard?" Daphne started singing, *really* badly. *"They will always love you!"*

"Wow." I rubbed my ears as if they were about to fall off. "Promise me you don't take this guy on a karaoke date. Just some friendly advice."

Daphne hopped onto the chair with a wooden spoon in her hand. "I'll have you know I'm great at karaoke! We should go some time!"

"Could be fun," I smirked, "I might have to get some earplugs first."

After we finished tidying up Daphne left, and I went upstairs to the apartment to start enjoying my evening off. Almost as soon as I walked through the front door the flamingo phone started ringing.

"Who is it?" I asked Phoebe as I walked over to the phone. Looking over I realized she was asleep. "Never mind then..." I picked up the phone. "Hello?"

"I hear my magic doll did a good job of keeping you safe," Mistress Bridgette said.

"Bridgette! I've been looking for you everywhere! Where did you go?"

After Blake and I apprehended Maddie I'd gone over to Bridgette's shop, only to find that it was completely gone. There was no sign of Bridgette or her voodoo bakery. "Let's just say my purpose in town was fulfilled. I will be back again—when the moment is right."

"I owe you an apology," I said. "I knew you were hiding something from me, I just figured it was a bad thing. Turns out you… came here in secret to protect me?" I guessed; still unsure what Bridgette's motivations were.

"I've got a priestess friend who has visions. She saw you in one of them. Said a powerful white witch needed voodoo protection. So, I came here and gave it to you. I couldn't really be upfront about it—voodoo requires a certain degree of secrecy."

"You told me all along that voodoo was white magic. I should have believed you. I do have a question though, why leave?"

"Your soul is surrounded with interesting color, Zora Wick. I sense a lot of danger on your path, but I sense a lot of allies too. I'm just one friend on the journey, others will come to your aid too—my time here is done for now, but the powers that be might bring be back one day."

"Well… I thank you again," I said. "I'd probably be a goner if it wasn't for you. I'm a little torn up about your sudden departure though, I was starting to get addicted to those sandwiches."

Bridgette laughed down the phone. "Tell you what, I'll send a recipe in the mail. Look after yourself Zora Wick, I think your world is only going to get more interesting…"

* * *

THE NEXT MORNING the intercom buzzed as I ate breakfast. "Hello?" I asked.

"Zora," Blake said and took a breath. "It's not a date, just two friends doing something fun. Message me your answer. If it's no… then throw it in the trash and forget this ever happened."

"What are you talking about?" I asked, feeling utterly confused. There was no response on the buzzer, so I went downstairs to the back door. There was no sign of Blake, but I found a box with a pair of ice-skates inside, along with two tickets and a note. *"This Friday, 8pm. Compass Cove Ice Rink. Not a date—unless you want it to be – Blake."*

I couldn't help but smiling as I held the note in my hands. I'd casually mentioned to Blake that I'd always wanted to go ice-skating, and it turned out he'd been listening. I took the things inside, pulled my phone out and message him.

"Very ice of you. Can't wait. See you there."

A second later he messaged back. *"On second thoughts I'm cancelling. That pun was awful."*

Smiling to myself I put my phone back in my pocket and practically floated on air for the rest of the morning. Zelda stopped around later in the morning with a Victoria sponge cake that she had baked from scratch.

"Don't judge it," she said as she set the cake down on the table. "I'm not a cake baker like you are."

"It looks great!" I said with as much support as I could. In truth the cake was leaning to one side, and it looked like a Great Dane had sat on it—but it was the thought that counted. "I think Ethyl is going to love it."

The plan was very simple. Zelda had baked a cake for the librarian so we could try and get back on her 'good books' and have our ban terminated. I'd offered to help and bake the cake for her, but Zelda insisted she was the one that had to do it. *"Trust me, it's the only way."*

We took the cake over to the library and accessed the magical library via the hidden passage. I felt like a naughty school child as we gingerly approached the front reception desk. Ethyl looked up from a huge book with old yellow pages and glared at us.

"You've both got some nerve coming back here!" she snapped.

"Here are all the overdue books on my account," Zelda said, pointing to a small suitcase on wheels that I had pulled here.

"All?" Ethyl scrutinized.

"Well… three are missing. I don't know where they are, but I'll find them. I promise!"

Ethyl pursed her lips. "What's in the box?"

"I made your favorite! ...again. Victoria Sponge, completely from scratch. No magic!"

Zelda set the box down and opened it, revealing the lopsided Victoria Sponge.

The head librarian considered the cake for a few long moments before nodding her head and smiling. "It's your worst one yet, but very well. I revoke the ban and reinstate your membership."

"Oh, thank you!" Zelda said and dropped to her knees. It was a tad dramatic in my opinion, but the library seemed to be a *very* big deal for my sister.

"It's not all sprinkles and rainbows, Zelda Wick," Ethyl said. "I'm moving you down to a Gold-level Bookworm. You'll have to work to get back up to Emerald."

"I can do it!" Zelda said determinedly. "I promise, I won't let you down!"

"Very good. Now... go and get a coffee. I need to talk to your sister in private."

Zelda looked at me in bafflement. "Her?!"

"Yes, now get out of here before I reinstate that ban."

"I'm going, I'm going!" Zelda shrieked as she hurried off.

"I'm sorry about breaking into the restricted section," I began, "It really was an accident."

"Accident or not, it was remarkably stupid," Ethyl dismissed. "But... it also shows that you are an extremely capable witch. Do you know what kind of security systems we have protecting that restricted section? There are probably only five witches in the entire world that could break into somewhere like that—so imagine my surprise when a beginner witch stumbles in without even breaking a sweat."

"It won't happen again, I promise."

"You seem like a woman of good character, so I'd be inclined to believe you. The fact of the matter however is that you are a Wick, and the women in your family have a penchant for mischief."

"...No comment."

"Here's the thing, successfully breaking into the restricted section in the first place is kind of a sign that a witch can handle stuff on the other side. But I'm not going to let you loose in there unsupervised. That's just asking for trouble."

"Agreed."

"So, I'm going to propose a deal. Help me out with a small problem and I'll give you supervised access to the restricted section. I've heard the rumors about you being a Prismatic Witch, are they true?"

I nodded. "Yes."

"Then you can help me."

"What's the problem?" I asked.

"It's a minor magical inconvenience, shouldn't be much for a witch like you. We'll arrange a proper meeting to go over the details next week. In the meantime, however, I thought you might want this." Ethyl reached under the table and handed me a list of book titles, some of the titles had been redacted.

"What is this?" I asked.

"Those are some of the last books your mother took out from the restricted section before she disappeared. Seems she was mighty interested in studying the mirror dimension—I don't know if that is any use to you."

I froze as I heard the words. I didn't know what the 'mirror dimension' was, but only a few weeks ago I was almost certain I'd seen my mother's reflection in the mirror of my bathroom! "I think it is useful, thank you."

"Alright then," Ethyl said and offered up a rare smile. "Now get out of here, I'll be in touch with regards to that favor. Tell Zelda to find those missing books as well."

"Will do, thanks!"

I found Zelda at the coffee shop, exchanging terrible puns with Jerry the rock golem. "Thanks Jerry, you're one in a million!" she shouted as I pulled her away. "I really shouldn't take you for granite!"

Once we were outside again, I relayed what had gone down with Ethyl, and I showed Zelda the list of books mom had borrowed.

"Woah, okay… I guess I owe you an apology," Zelda said. "Looks like mom might be trapped in your mirror after all. The mirror dimension? Bloody hell mom."

"What is the mirror dimension?" I asked. "Is it dangerous?"

"It's uh... how do I put this? It's probably just about the most dangerous magical thing I can think of. If she was messing around with this stuff, then no wonder she disappeared! We should probably show this to Liza..."

As we stepped outside the library a familiar face was there waiting for us.

"Hudson!" I remarked. "What are you doing here?"

"I uh..." he paused and looked at Zelda. "Can I have a word alone with you a moment?"

Zelda rolled her eyes and huffed dramatically. "I'll meet you back at the shop, Zora!" she said as she stomped down the library's front steps.

"So, what's up?" I asked Hudson.

"So, this job has come up, and I kind of *have* to take it. Only thing is that it's pretty dangerous."

"How dangerous are we talking here?"

"Uh... fifty percent chance that I'm going to die and never come back," he said, scratching the back of his head.

"What?! So don't take it then!"

"I really don't have a choice. Sometimes things come up, and if I don't handle them then things will be *much* worse."

"There are other agents, aren't there? Let them handle it!"

"...I'm kind of the best one. I'm not bragging. Three other agents have already died trying to handle this thing."

"Well, what is it?"

"I can't tell you that, it's classified."

I stared at Hudson for a moment. "Why did you come here to tell me this?"

"Because my director advised me to get my affairs in order before I go. There's something I've been wanting to do, and if I die without doing it, I'm going to be one grumpy ass ghost."

I shook my head as I waited for the answer. "Alright then, so what is it?"

Without warning he took my head in his hands and kissed me. It didn't last much longer than five seconds, but in those five seconds my world came crashing to a halt. When Hudson pulled away everything was spinning. I felt dizzy and breathless.

"I'm sorry," he said. "I should have asked first."

"No, it's..." I said, though I was lost in some sort of daze. I couldn't get the words out of my mouth properly.

"I have to go," he said as he turned to leave. "Bye Zora."

Hudson started walking down the steps when I shouted after him. "Hey!" He turned around. "You don't get to do that to me and then possibly just walk away forever. If you die on this mission then I'm going to kill you, do you understand?"

Hudson looked at me with the most puzzled expression on his face. "Uh... yes? In a very weird way."

"Good. Just so we're clear then. Goodbye. Don't die."

His eyes twinkled in an amused way. "I'll be back. I promise."

With that I watched Hudson walk down the steps, possibly for the last time. Would he return? Would I ever see him again?

Only time would tell.

CLICK HERE to read Book 4: Cookies N' Scream

THANKS FOR READING

Thanks for reading, I hope you enjoyed the book.

It would really help me out if you could leave an honest review with your thoughts and rating on Amazon.

Every bit of feedback helps!

ALSO BY MARA WEBB

~ Ongoing ~

Hallow Haven Witch Mysteries

An English Enchantment

Compass Cove Cozy Mysteries

~ Completed ~

Wicked Witches of Pendle Island

Wildes Witches Mysteries

Raven Bay Mysteries

Wicked Witches of Vanish Valley

MAILING LIST

Want to be notified when I release my latest book? Join my mailing list. It's for new releases only. No spam:

Click here to join!

I'll also send you a free 120,000 word book as a thank you for signing up.

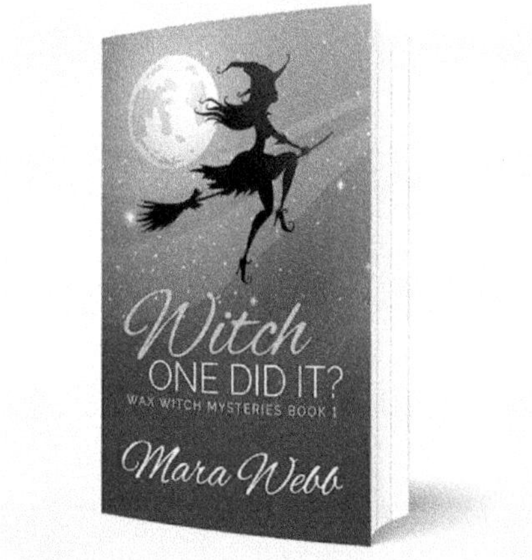

marawebbauthor.com

amazon.com/-/e/B081X754NL
facebook.com/marawebbauthor
twitter.com/marawebbauthor
bookbub.com/authors/mara-webb